The Black Jewel Case

by G. H. Teed

First published in the Union Jack,
2nd Series, No. 518, 13 September 1913.

Illustrated by Val Reading

Stillwoods Edition

Stillwoods.Blogspot.Ca

Catalogue Information:
Title: The Black Jewel Case
Author: G. H. Teed (1881-1938)
First published in the Union Jack, 2nd Series, No. 518, 13 September
1913.
Illustrated by: Val Reading.
This Edition by: Stillwoods, 2021
ISBN Canada: 978-1-989788-43-1
Blog: Stillwoods.Blogspot.Ca
Author Blog: http://ghteed.blogspot.com/
Storefront: http://www.lulu.com/spotlight/lulubook22

Keywords: Sexton Blake, British fictional detective, Tinker, Yvonne
Cartier

Cautionary Note: This series of books by Stillwoods are
intended to make the stories of G. H. Teed, born in New Brunswick,
Canada, available to collectors and researchers. The editor, or rather
digitizer has not altered the original publication.

This story may contain language and racial terms that are not
appropriate to today. I apologize for them; I know that the author was
using his voice to excite and entertain an adventurous English
audience. These works were published from 82 to 110 years ago.
Most every work has characters of redeeming ethnicity within.

I hope you enjoy and share these stories; I have.
Doug Frizzle

Tinker is nearly captured by Yvonne.
A Charming Romance of Yvonne and Sexton Blake

THE Honourable Algernon Montague Bayes was hunched up gloomily in the big leather chair in the smoking-room of the Junior Exchange Club, staring out unseeingly at the sun-grilled street and the passers-by, whose summery attire testified to the power of the solar smile reserved for London during the month of August. In his hand he held a half crumpled letter, and from the fierce grasp of that same white hand, it was evident that the letter was the cause of his depressed attitude. But for a silent waiter, who hovered about in the classic atmosphere at the far end, and who, in spite of the dignified surroundings, paused every now and then to thoughtfully scratch a mole under his left ear, the Honourable Algernon had the whole room to himself.

When fifteen minutes had gone by and he had not ordered a drink—a marvellous piece of forgetfulness on his part—the waiter moved by silent strategy until his expansive countenance was within the range of vision of the gloomy-looking member. The waiter's tactics were successful, for his presence roused the Honourable Algy from his absorption, and without lifting his head he said:

"Waitah!"

"Yessir?"

"A whisky-and-soda."

"Yessir."

"And waitah!"

"Yessir?"

"Make it stiff."

"Yessir."

"Not too much soda."

"Nozir."

"And waitah!"

"Yessir?"

"Did you evah—er—get taken down, waitah —spoofed—nipped?"

"Yessir."

"Ah! You did?"

"Yessir."

"What was your sensation, waitah?"

"I felt empty like, sir."

"Was it for much, waitah?"

"'Arf-a-sovereign, sir."

"Half-a—oh lor'! Bring me that drink, waitah!"

"Yessir."

As the man hurried away, the Honourable Algy relapsed once more into his gloomy thoughts, muttering:

"Half-a-sovereign! Good heavens! And he remembers it. And I've lost the half of fifty thousand sovereigns!—Ruined—smashed—busted clean! Shades of Artaxerxes—half-a-sovereign!"

When his drink arrived, he once more roused himself and turned gloomily to it. He had consumed less than half of it when a figure appeared through the doorway which led into the library, and took his way languidly down the room, until he reached the Honourable Algy.

The newcomer was over medium height, and middle-aged. His silvering beard and moustache were trimmed with scrupulous exactitude, his suit of tropical grey a credit to his tailor, his boots immaculate, his whole appearance quietly elegant. He was evidently on familiar terms with the younger man, who cocked a gloomy eye at him, for he smiled slightly and sank into a seat beside him.

Signing to the waiter to approach, he ordered a bottle of soda. Then he turned to the other.

"What's up, Algy? You look as though you'd been thrown over."

"Worse than that, Graves." replied the other, "I'm stumped—clean bowled!"

"Oh, it can't be as bad as that!" drawled the other, "Been backing the gee-gees?"

"No, worse, in me Graves, you see a perfect example of the boob, the gazoo, the yahoo, the one and only easy mark for sharks. That kid out in the road is a Solomon compared with me. I'm the only Simon, pure, unadulterated brand of gink out of captivity!"

"Great Scott! Algy, it must be of a serious nature to affect you like that!"

"It is—it is!" groaned the other. "Dash it! I'll have to go to work now, and I haven't the ghost of an idea how to set about it."

"What is it, anyway?" smiled Graves, as he thought of the Honourable Algy toiling behind a desk. "Perhaps you are overestimating its seriousness."

"No chance of that. Here, Graves, read that. You'll see for yourself that it's serious enough."

Graves put out his hand and took the letter. Then deliberately adjusting his pince-nez, he lifted it up and read. It was headed:

"Letter to the Shareholders of the Golden Princess Mining Company.

"Dear Sir —It is with deep regret that we have to inform you, on behalf of the directors of the Golden Princess Mine, that expectations, which were based on the engineer's report, have not been realised. You may remember that in the last report issued, a detailed account was given of the work being proceeded with on the thousand-foot level. It was confidently anticipated that a cross-cut from this depth would disclose a rich saddle formation, which, by all appearances, seemed to exist.

"Unfortunately, expectations were not realised, the shaft, after much labour, only running into barren quartz. To complicate matters, the mine has been making water so fast that a special pumping plant would have to be installed in order to cope with it.

"As you know, all the available funds of the company have been expended in machinery and operating expenses, and if further operations were to be undertaken, the capitalisation of the company would have to be increased. At a meeting of the directors yesterday, it was considered that the prospects did not warrant this action, and by unanimous vote it was decided to abandon operations.

"So consistently disappointing have results been that, after the most careful deliberations, it has been decided that affairs must be placed in the hands of a receiver. As solicitors to the company, we could not possibly advise any other course.

"We had anticipated that we would be able to hold out the promise of a dividend after matters had been settled, but an examination of the accounts shows that outstanding claims will exhaust all that we can hope to realise on the machinery and other assets.

"Being heavy losers ourselves, we can sympathise with any chagrin you may feel regarding the unsuccessful outcome of the venture. However, it will be our one endeavour to discover a highly profitable enterprise for your consideration in the near future, which, we hope, will not only reimburse you for any loss you may have sustained from the failure of the Golden Princess Mine, but pay you a handsome profit in addition.

"All notices and reports of further developments relating to the above mine will be posted to you in due course.

"We are, dear Sir,

"Your obedient servants,

"GREEN & SMART.

"To The Honourable Algernon Montague Bayes, Junior Exchange Club, Piccadilly."

When Graves finished reading he laid the letter on his knee, took off his pince-nez, and regarded his companion as though he were examining a new specimen of the genus homo.

"Well, Algy," he finally drawled, "I quite agree with you. You are everything you called yourself, and more. What, in the name of all that's wonderful, possessed you to have any dealings with Green & Smart? They are the biggest sharks in this big city!"

"Oh, dash it! I know it now when it's too late, Graves. I went to see Harland on 'Change as soon as I got the letter, and he told me the same. Says I'll never get a penny back— that they are rank swindlers, and that this is an old game of theirs."

"Did you lose much?"

"Every golden disc I had in the world."

"Whew! They did land you for fair, Algy. Do you mind telling me the amount?"

"Twenty-five thousand."

"What mirth there will be in the swindler's den over that! What on earth possessed you to risk all you had on a gold-mine, above all things?"

"Well, I —er —well, Graves, I was thinking it was time for me to —er —settle down. Green held out such alluring promises that I couldn't withstand them. Swore I'd double my money in six months."

"So you have —backwards," remarked Graves drily. "Ye gods! Twenty-five thousand—and with Green & Smart. It's unbelievable!"

"I suppose Harland is right when he says I haven't the ghost of a chance of getting it back?"

"My dear Algy, you could collect it quicker from the waiter. Green & Smart are the slipperiest gentlemen in the business. If there is anything in the game of legalised swindle which they don't know it is only because they haven't had time to think it up yet. You've got about as much chance of realising as a wooden-legged man would have in passing the Army test. Besides, you may wager what little they left you that they are fully protected by this intricate and comprehensive law of ours. No, my boy; there is just one thing for you to do —swallow it. Perhaps the lady will wait for you."

The Honourable Algy groaned, then sat up and set his jaw in a way which was new to him.

"By heavens, Graves, I'll swallow it! There's nothing else to do. But I swear if I ever get those slimy crooks where I want 'em, I'll show 'em I don't intend to take it lying down. I know I'm not as clever as some people," he added bitterly, "but I trusted them—trusted them as men of honour!"

"Algy, they don't know the meaning of the word. It doesn't exist in any lexicon which they use. You have one consolation, and that is, you are not alone. Messrs. Green & Smart have a particular weakness for defrauding the widow and orphan. They do well at it, too, I can assure you. Green's wife is one of the most blatant exhibits of the combined art of the jeweller, the modiste, and the milliner you could find in a day's journey. By the same means do they run a lavish establishment in the City and a big place in the country."

"I wish I could discover some way of getting back at them, Graves. If I could I wouldn't mind so much."

"Good heavens!"

"What s the matter?"

"Don't speak to me for a few minutes, Algy. Let me think. By Jove, I wonder if she would. It would appeal to her immensely."

"Wonder who would what? What would appeal to who? And who is 'she,' Graves?"

"Algy, finish that drink and come with me. I've got an idea which may put you in the way of getting back some of your money."

"What's the idea, Graves?" asked the other eagerly. "What plan has occurred to you?"

"Not a word yet. Don't build any hopes on it, Algy. You'll know in good time. Come along."

Gulping down his drink, and with a wondering look in his eyes, the Honourable Algernon Montague Bayes rose, settled his waistcoat, lit a cigarette, and followed his guide. Graves led the way from the club to the street. There an ivory-coloured motor was waiting, and into this he motioned his companion. Stepping after he said "home," and leaned back.

Along Piccadilly the car rolled silently, then the chauffeur turned, and by quiet streets drove along until he reached Queen Anne's Gate.

"Come on, Algy," said Graves, as the car drew into the kerb before a quietly imposing block of flats.

"I'm hanged if I can see your idea, Graves!"

"Never mind, you'll see soon enough."

Graves ran up the steps and turned to the right. Pausing before a heavy door which gave entrance to one of the flats, he inserted a key and stood aside for his companion to enter.

Though the place was designated a flat it was more of a house than anything else, from the point of view of the number of rooms. Luxuriously furnished with rich hangings and soft carpets, it was a monument of perfect taste.

The entrance hall was big and square, and struck a restful note, which was sustained by the reception-room into which Graves ushered his guest. A big door revealed a vista of other rooms, which harmonised delightfully with the rest, and as the Honourable Algernon sank into a chair, with a sigh, he gazed around him with pleasure.

"My word, Graves, you have got scrumptious digs! Live here all alone?"

Graves laughed.

"No, my boy. My niece is the mistress of the house. It is to see her that I brought you here. Wait a few moments, and I'll see if she is at home."

Before the astonished visitor could reply Graves was gone. Five minutes passed before the curtains over the door were lifted and Graves returned, accompanied by a girl. The Honourable Algy so far forgot the inborn tenets of his ancient family as literally to gape at the beautiful girl who entered, then, with an embarrassed flush, he stumbled to his feet and bowed as Graves made the introduction.

The girl smiled and held out her hand, her easy manner making the young man forget his embarrassment. Then she sat down, and chatted banalities until tea was brought in. When a man-servant, with a decidedly nautical cut about him, had served it and retired, Graves turned to the girl and said:

"I brought Mr. Bayes up to see you for a certain reason, Yvonne. He's had a rough experience with Messrs. Green & Smart —in fact, they have succeeded in robbing him of twenty-five thousand."

"I'm very sorry to hear that, uncle. Surely you must have been

6

ignorant of their standing, Mr. Bayes?"

"I was, mademoiselle." Then turning to Graves, he added: "Really, Graves, I don't see why we should burden Mademoiselle Cartier with my worries."

"You wait," drawled Graves. "I brought you here for a purpose. I presume you are still anxious to get back your money?"

"Naturally."

"Then do as you're told, my boy. I want you to repeat all you told me. In fact, let us have the full details for mademoiselle's benefit."

"Yes, do," put in Yvonne. "We may be able to think of something which will enable us to get your money back."

"Well," laughed the Honourable Algernon, with embarrassment, "I don't exactly see the point. How you or your uncle can assist me, I can't imagine. Won't it be boring to listen to it?"

"Not at all," smiled Yvonne. "Please tell me all."

"All right," laughed the young man, with a faint tinge of nervousness. "It all began about three months ago—in fact, soon after my governor's death. I'm a second son, mademoiselle, and when the governor died he left me twenty-five thousand. That was quite enough for me to live on alone, but —er —the truth is that lately I —er — thought of getting married. Naturally, my income was not sufficient to set up the kind of establishment marriage would entail, so, before asking the lady, I —er —thought I'd see if I couldn't make some more. Lots of chaps I know seem to do pretty well in the City, so I didn't see why I shouldn't.

"As bad luck would have it, I was introduced to Solomon Green just about then, and —well, the upshot was, I fell a prey to his oily tongue. According to his tale, he had the greatest gold prospect in existence. It was situated in Australia, and only needed a hundred thousand to purchase machinery and start operations when returns would start coming in. We were all going to double our money in six months, and treble it in twelve.

"Of course, I don't know any more about a gold mine than a Hottentot knows about the Stock Exchange. I had heard and read of mining frauds, but such a thing in connection with Green never entered my mind. At any rate, I plunked down every penny I had, and began at once to reckon just how much interest my money would return me in six months, and how wealthy I should be in two years. Right up until a week ago Green assured me that things were going swimmingly; then, like a bombshell, comes this letter."

Here the Honourable Algy drew out the letter which he had shown to Graves, and passed it across to Yvonne. Silence reigned while she perused it, but as soon as she laid it down Bayes continued his narration. All shyness had departed, in the greater grip of his indignation, and he picked out the necessary facts, discarding the unimportant ones with a judgment new to him.

"I got that this morning," he went on, "and, if you will pardon the expression, mademoiselle, it completely took the wind out of my sails. For a time I was too dazed to think, much less act, but finally I put on my hat, left the club, and took a taxi to the City. There I looked up Harland, of Harland & Bruce, and told him the whole thing. He read the letter, and then —well, I'm afraid I couldn't repeat verbatim what he did say, but he talked straight.

"I gathered that this kind of thing was an old game of Green's. Harland says they have been doing it for years, and confine their operations to widows and men like myself, who know nothing of business. He also says that they know every kink in the law, and though case after case has been started against them, it has been impossible to catch them napping.

"It seems that they have a lot of old mining machinery, which is worthless. When they promote a mine they have an interest in it, and naturally, as all the shareholders of their ventures are equally ignorant, all the management is left to Green & Smart. In addition to controlling the company, they appoint themselves solicitors of it, and Green & Smart as directors, advised by Green & Smart as solicitors, decide what shall be done.

"Then they sell this old machinery to the company at a high price —many times over what it is worth. They don't pay cash to themselves for it, and, of course, it is owned under a dummy name. They are too shrewd for that. The dummy owner accepts as payment a first mortgage on the property. Then operations begin. Of course, Green & Smart cook up fake expenditures, charging them to operation expenses.

"After a while the prospect peters out, the 'owner' of the machinery demands that the mortgage be taken up, there is no money, and as a result the mine goes into the hands of a receiver, and Green & Smart apparently lose like the other shareholders. The creditors make their claims, are paid, and in due course the money, or the

8

greater part of it, filters back to the capacious pockets of Green & Smart.

"That, mademoiselle, is the situation. I am sorry to have worried you with a lot of uninteresting details concerning my affairs, and I really can't see why your uncle insisted I should tell you."

"On the contrary, Mr. Hayes, I have been deeply interested in your narrative. Men like Messrs. Green & Smart are exactly the type of men I enjoy meeting —on occasion. Do you mind if I ask you a few questions?"

"Not at all. I shall be delighted to answer any that I can."

"Thank you. I gather from this letter of Green & Smart's, that a receiver has not yet been appointed?"

"That is correct."

"Consequently the mine is technically still a going concern?"

"Yes."

"And even now a transfer of shares would be legally correct?"

"Yes," smiled the young man; "but I don't think there is any danger of that occurring."

"I'm not so sure," replied Yvonne coolly, "How much would you take for your interest?"

"I beg your pardon?"

"How much would you take for your interest?"

"Nothing, mademoiselle. I wouldn't sell worthless paper of that description to a fellow being, for the only purchaser would be one ignorant of the true state of affairs."

"I am not."

"No, of course not; but you are not a prospective purchaser. Before I sold them to anybody I should tell them the true facts, and then, of course, only an insane person would buy them."

"Do I look insane?"

"Good heavens, no!"

"You are quite prepared to consider me as in my right and proper mind?"

"Well, of course," cried the bewildered fellow, gazing in amazement at Yvonne's smiling eyes.

"All right, Mr. Bayes. I'll make you an offer for your shares in the —er —Golden Princess Mining Company."

"Oh, you are joking, mademoiselle."

"And the price I offer," went on Yvonne, not heeding his remark, "is what you paid —twenty-five thousand pounds."

"Now I know you are joking."

"On the contrary, I never was more serious in my life. By the way, what is the par value of them?"

"Fifty thousand pounds. Green said they would be at par in six months."

"Well, what is your answer? Will you sell them to me?"

"It pleases you to jest," said the Honourable Algernon, a trifle stiffly. "It is not of a humorous nature to me."

"I am not jesting," said, Yvonne quietly. "Uncle, will you be so good as to get my cheque-book? It is in the top drawer in the desk in my room."

"Certainly," smiled Graves, rising and departing.

While he was gone Yvonne sat studying the toe of her shoe, while the Honourable Algernon gazed moodily at the carpet, wondering what kind of a practical joke Graves was putting up on him, and how far they intended carrying it. More than once he glanced at the door as though tempted to make his exit, but a hidden strain of stubbornness in the young fellow held him there, determined to see it out, despite his desire to be alone with his worry.

For, to him, the future was dark. Not that he didn't have the pluck to turn out and work. Underneath his drawling exterior he had good stuff in him, and the great trouble lay in the fact that he didn't know how to work. Like many other young men of his class, he had never been taught how to take care of himself, the result being that when disaster did come he was as helpless as a child.

Humanity is divided into two classes—producers and spenders. One lives on the efforts of the other, and though, under our complicated system of civilisation, grades and classes are a necessity, the balance of things would be much better maintained were each man a producer in some way.

Business does not lessen the dignity of a peer or an earl. On the contrary, the entry of such men into business dignifies commerce, lends an impetus to that element, and gives encouragement to the great army of producers, without which humanity would sink back into a savage state. Consequently, it was not the Honourable Algy's fault that the loss of his money left him so helpless, but rather the fault of the system under which he had been reared.

He was still moodily pondering when Graves returned, and his expression did not change when Yvonne took the cheque-book, crossed to a small rosewood desk, and calmly seated herself. Picking up a pen, she filled in a cheque form, and pushed the book away from her.

Then she rose and walked across to her seat.

"Mr. Bayes," she said, with a smile, "I have in my hand my own cheque for twenty-five thousand pounds. It is quite regular in every way, and I think you will find it will be paid at once on presentation. Once more I offer you this amount for your interest in the gold mine. I give you my word that I am not jesting. I am perfectly serious. Will you accept it?"

"But—but," he stammered, "I couldn't! That would be dishonest. The shares are utterly worthless. Perhaps, mademoiselle, you are not well versed in business matters, and did not quite gather my meaning?"

Graves burst out laughing.

"Algy, you'll be the death of me," he drawled, "My dear fellow, she knows more about the intricacies of the share market than half the men on 'Change. You accept her offer."

"But, Graves, don't you see I can't? It would be giving no value for the money. If it is only offered in order to help me out —well —er —pardon me, but I am not in need of charity,"

"There is no question of that," broke in Yvonne. "Listen. Mr. Bayes. My offer to you is serious, as I have said. I know that the shares are worthless, and always will be. My reasons for purchasing them are twofold—one, because you have become entangled in a web which you are helpless to break, and the other is my desire to pit my wits against Messrs. Green & Smart. You are evidently not aware that I have some little —er —reputation for such things.

"True, it is all a gamble on my part, but if I can't get that twenty-five thousand back from Green & Smart I'll consider the money well spent in gaining a new experience. I owe my Uncle my thanks for bringing your case to my notice, for I have sworn enmity against all and sundry who prey on their fellow beings, be it the wealthy shark who catches big fish, or the man who sweats the lives out of poor flower-makers in the slums."

"Good heavens! Are you *the* Mademoiselle Yvonne?" gasped the young man.

"I must plead guilty," smiled Yvonne.

For fully a minute he stared at her in stupefaction, then he leaned back and laughed.

"Well, I am a ninny. I thought Graves was pulling my— er— foot, and that you were doing likewise. I apologise for my doubt. Will you really help me?" he added eagerly.

"That is exactly what I am offering to do," replied Yvonne. "In order to do so, however, I want your interest in the company. I have the germ of an idea in my mind as to how I shall induce Messrs. Green & Smart to part with twenty-five thousand pounds, and that amount of interest in the mine is necessary in order to carry it out."

"Then I accept your offer, I needn't say how gladly. However, I shall bank the money, and will only permit you to assist me on condition that you promise to let me pay the money back to you if you fail to get it from Green & Smart."

Yvonne nodded.

"I am quite agreeable to that," she said. "How soon can you get the shares?"

"Oh, now if necessary!"

"Very well, uncle, you go along with Mr. Bayes and arrange about the transfer. Take the cheque with you, and give it to him there. We must lose no time in doing this, for the mine will probably be put into the receiver's hands almost at once."

"Right-ho," grinned Graves, "Come along, Algy, we'll fix things up right away."

The young man rose, and held out his hand to Yvonne.

"I'm sure I don't know how to thank you, mademoiselle," he said huskily. "I feel a cad, letting you run this risk for me, and I wouldn't do it only on the condition I named."

"Just forget all about it," answered Yvonne kindly. "The next time know with whom you are dealing before you risk your money with them."

"I will; indeed I will," he replied fervently.

When he and Graves had departed, Yvonne stood and laughed softly to herself.

"Oh! it will do me good to cross swords with those sharks. It is risky, and perhaps a trifle outside the letter of the law, but it can't be helped. It is that same law which permits the existence of carrion like Green & Smart. It is that law which permitted my mother and myself to fall victims to the same type of schemes in Australia. They are continually elaborating it in order to give greater protection to the public, and so unwieldy has it become, that a clever man can do a lot which is morally wrong, and yet not be answerable to it.

"And on the strength of this do creatures like Green & Smart exist, making war on helpless women and inexperienced young fellows like Bayes. Heigho! If I do run foul of the law, I suppose I'll have to do some dodging. Never-mind; it will be exciting, anyway, and unless Sexton Blake enters the field against me, I defy them to put their fingers on me."

As she murmured Blake's name Yvonne's eyes grew dreamy with thoughts of the past, then, with a little laugh, she shook herself and turned to leave the room.

She made her way along until she reached the library. There she knelt down before a small safe, and, after setting the letter combination, she turned the handle and opened the door. On the top shelf was a long black case, bound in leather. This she drew out and carried to the desk.

Seating herself, she picked up the case, and after a few moments' manipulation, her fingers pressed a hidden spring and the cover flew up. Inside was a magnificent necklace of diamonds, and lifting it out, she held it up.

The stones caught the light in a thousand hues and scintillated like living fire, the predominating "blue" stamping them as the rarest and most valuable of all diamonds. In the centre was one great stone of unrivalled purity, whose value alone must have been enormous.

From this the stones graded out on either side until they tapered down close to the clasp to the size of a pea. As a thing of value it was worth a fortune, and as an article of adornment, it was fit to grace the throat of an empress.

Yvonne let the stones slip caressingly through her hands, then she returned it to the case and closed the cover with a snap. Once again she pressed the same secret spring, and the cover flew up to reveal — nothing.

The inside was the same, the white satin lining, the raised centre around which the necklace was arranged, but of the necklace there was absolutely no sign. Its apparent disappearance seemed not to worry Yvonne, however, for she laughed softly, and was just rising to put it away when Graves came in.

"You weren't long, uncle."

"No. We drove to Algy's place in the car and fixed things up at once."

"You got the certificates, then?"

"Oh, yes; here they are."

Drawing out a package of folded certificates, whose borders were the only "gilt-edged" thing about the Golden Princess Mine, Graves tossed them on the desk.

"Scott! he's the most pleased young man in London. I didn't dream, however, that you would enter into the thing so quickly, Yvonne. I only brought him up to see if you could suggest something."

"Oh, that's all right! I could see at once what methods they had used, I'm glad you brought him."

"What is your plan?"

Yvonne held the black jewel-case.

"Do you see this?"

"I'm not blind."

"Well, this case is going to be my instrument in the matter."

"I don't follow you."

"Listen! and I will tell you."

Then Yvonne bent over and spoke rapidly, and as Graves listened, he chuckled delightedly.

A CHARMING STUDY OF YVONNE BY "VAL."

September 13th, 1913.

MR. SOLOMON GREEN was corpulent, bald-headed, and possessed an oily smile. His dark Hebraic eyes surmounted a pronounced Semitic nose, which curved over a heavy black moustache as though to restrain it upon the thick, heavy lip which it adorned. His hands were fat and podgy, and the fingers of each were loaded with diamond rings, so large and numerous as to be vulgarly vulgar, so blatant as to proclaim to all that Mr. Solomon Green was a man who had "arrived."

The office in which he sat was typical of himself —overdone in most things, yet luxurious in a certain way. Its obvious purpose would be self-evident to the keen eyes of one initiated into the wiles and ways of the "City," but to the inexperienced vision of timid widows and callow youths who were Mr. Solomon Green's chief prey, it presented an appearance of solidity, inspiring them with confidence in the expansive figure of the Jew who loomed, white-waistcoated, before them.

On the morning on which he enters this record, he had just finished reading his letters, and had leaned back with a smile of satisfaction. For one of his most successful coups—the floating of the Golden Princess Mine—had been brought to a highly satisfying end, and that most of his letters contained complaints, threats, pleadings, cries of ruin and bitter denunciation in reply to his last circular regarding the mine, it bothered Solomon Green not at all.

He was fully aware of the fact that there was a fool born every minute, and he considered himself as appointed by destiny to deal with as many as possible, his chief regret being that he could not add to his harvest by taking under his wing a still larger proportion.

He knew where he stood and how much thought it was necessary to waste on the more threatening of his correspondents. Mr. Green was too thorough a master of the game to make any mistakes which might later recoil on him. He knew to the finest detail just what to do and how to do it, and Graves summed him up as well as possible when he told the Honourable Algernon that, if there were any points in the game of legalised robbery unknown to the firm of Green and Smart, it was only because they hadn't had time to think them up.

In the old days, before Mr. Green had achieved anything like his present wealth, and when a solitary diamond adorned his right hand, he was shunned like the plague by those who knew. Now, however, his money had furnished the golden key which unlocked many doors through which it was his ambition to enter, and with its usual capacity, "society" had swallowed the gilded pill —or pills —in the form of Solomon Green and his wife.

Though he was sure of his ground, he never made the mistake of not keeping his hand on the pulse of those whom he had rooked. His replies were masterpieces of suave regret, and when he thought a second attempt safe, he placed before his victim another tempting dish, which, not infrequently, was consumed.

One letter which he had firmly expected had not arrived, however, and Mr. Solomon Green permitted a faint frown to appear on his smooth brow as he pondered on the matter.

"By all the rules," he muttered slowly, "the Honourable Algernon should have replied to the circular. If he had plenty more I could imagine him swallowing his loss, but, by his own statement, that twenty-five thousand was all he had, and I can't conceive of any man losing his whole 'roll' without making a 'holler.' Besides, he was the biggest shareholder in the mine —always excepting myself."

And as the thought flickered across his mind, Solomon Green smiled.

At that moment a knock came at the door, and a clerk entered bearing a few letters.

Laying them on the desk in front of Green, he withdrew. As the door closed, the Jew picked them up and tossed them one by one aside on seeing their non-importance.

At the very bottom of the pile, however, there was one which caught his attention, and turning it over, he saw what he expected — an embossed crest. With a faint smile he slit it open and drew out the sheet.

As he read the contents the smile left his face and the fine line in his brow deepened. It was, to say the least, hardly the kind of letter he had expected to receive from the Honourable Algy, whose signature was at the bottom.

"Dear Sirs," he read. "I am in receipt of your favour of the 10th instant, and note what you say regarding the Golden Princess Mine. My feelings of regret, however, are tempered by the fact that I have just disposed of my interest in the mine at the same figure which I paid, viz., twenty-five thousand pounds. If you would care for the name and address of the purchaser I should be pleased to forward same to you. Perhaps you will desire to send on a circular.

"It is pleasing to read that you are endeavouring to discover a profitable investment which will recoup the shareholders of the unlucky Golden Princess, and I wish you every success in your search. By all means forward me particulars when you have succeeded.

"Yours faithfully, ALGERNON MONTAGUE BAYES."

Solomon Green laid down the letter, and for five minutes cursed silently.

"If that isn't about the limit," he growled savagely. "Who on earth has been fool enough to buy those shares from Bayes? Is it another lamb like himself, or—Good heavens! is that seemingly brainless youth shrewder than I thought him? In any case, I must find out who it is, and prepare for squalls. He had them a week ago, I know. Anyway, if there is any row over the matter, Bayes is liable to the purchaser. I'll write him for the name and address. Then I'll send a circular and sit tight."

With that resolve he turned back to his desk, but once again was interrupted by the entry of a clerk. Approaching the desk he bent over and said in low tones:

"There's a lady outside wants to see you, sir. I told her I'd see if you were in."

"Ever seen her before?"

"No, sir. She's a stranger."

"Young or old?"

"Young, and a widow I imagine, from the way she is dressed."

"Ah! in that case send her in."

As the clerk withdrew, Green smoothed his brow and adopted the specially benevolent expression which he reserved for such callers.

A moment later the door opened, and he rose to greet a slim woman in widow's weeds, who walked slowly and timidly across the room.

"Are you Mr. Green —Mr. Solomon Green?" she asked in subdued tones, with just the hint of a nervous quaver in them.

"I am, madam," replied Green, looking sympathetic. "Won't you be seated?" And as his caller sank into a chair with murmured thanks, he coughed and said:

"You are —er —lately bereaved?"

The other made an inaudible sound which he took to be an acknowledgment of that fact.

"Ah! Yes, yes," he went on piously as he resumed his own seat, "in the midst of life we are in death. Still we must bear our sorrows with a cheerful mind."

"I try to," came the low tones from behind the heavy veil. "It is so hard, though, when one is left completely friendless and alone, knowing nothing of business nor how to invest one's wealth."

That word wealth was as balm to the soul of Solomon Green. To him it presented such a comforting vision of future possibilities, so much more promising than the word "money."

"True, true," he purred, "but, by diligent search men can be found who are capable of investing funds to the greatest advantage," and he swept his fat bediamonded hand about in a gesture which indicated that the office she was in was visible proof that such an individual existed in the person of Mr. Solomon Green.

"It is so comforting to know that, Mr. Green, for I have come to you for advice. I know you are a very busy man, but you will find time to advise me, won't you?"

Mr. Green looked properly dubious.

"Well," he said finally, "I am pretty busy, though I won't deny that you have come to the right man if you wish to invest your money. Still, I might advise you. Have you —er—"

"Much to invest?" finished his visitor. "Of course it would be very little to you, Mr. Green, but to me it is a lot, a hundred and fifty thousand altogether."

The Jew could hardly keep the quiver of joy from his tones as he replied:

"Not a fortune, madam, not a fortune, but a very respectable sum indeed. Properly invested it ought to yield you a very handsome income."

"Then you will advise me?" she asked eagerly.

"Have you no friends, brothers or relations to whom you could go?"

"None that I would care to deal with in this matter," she answered.

"In that case, madam, I am quite prepared to give you the benefit of my wisdom such as it is. Is your money available now?"

"Not immediately. It will be, however, in a week or ten days at the latest."

"Ah! Just time enough to look up something good for you. Is it in cash?"

"Yes."

"Excellent, that saves so much bother. Really, madam, I think I shall make a special point of looking after your affairs. Now, if you will favour me with a few details, we can discuss matters further."

"Certainly, anything you wish to know."

"Your name is?"

"Carter."

"And your address?"

"Temporarily the Hotel Knickerbocker."

"And your permanent address?"

"It was Australia. I shall find a place in Europe now."

"Widow of a wealthy squatter probably," he thought as he noted the particulars. "I shall have to change the location of my new mining schemes from Australia to South Africa." Then aloud he said:

"Thank you, Mrs. Carter. I shall begin at once to search for a suitable investment. Have you any particular fancy of your own?"

"N —no. Mines are rather profitable, aren't they?"

Once again a quiver of joy ran through Solomon Green.

"How curious," he smiled suavely. "I was just thinking myself that a good mining investment was the very thing for you. There is always an element of risk, of course, but it can be made infinitesimal."

"I'm sure you will find a suitable one," she murmured sweetly, throwing back her veil.

Green barely suppressed a gasp of amazement as he saw the beauty of his fair caller. He had been able to make out the vague outline of her features through the veil, and could see she was not ugly. He had been little prepared for the reality, however, and had he possessed any of the finer feelings he must have felt a tinge of regret as he gazed into those clear, deep azure eyes.

She looked little more than a girl, but her apparent youth and helplessness struck no responsive chord in the Jew's heart, beyond causing him to think, with an inward smirk, that he would contrive to have many interviews with his new client. Perhaps later a little dinner "a deux" at the Savoy, with the theatre and supper afterwards at Romano's. One never could tell.

Had he been as well informed regarding women's apparel as he was regarding sharp finance, he might have noticed that the wedding-ring which his visitor wore was new —blatantly new. It is all the more surprising in a way that he didn't, for no man in London possessed a more thorough knowledge of jewellery and precious stones than did the same Solomon Green, a knowledge gained in the Ghetto in his younger days, when he used to travel up and down the streets hawking his wares, which consisted of a few chip diamonds wrapped up in a piece of tissue paper.

The helpless attitude, the utter girlishness and the appealing beauty of his visitor, dulled any thought of suspicion, and he thanked his stars that such a Golconda had dropped out of the sky into his very hands.

As he finished making his notes, he looked up with a smile.

"Thank you, Mrs. Carter. I shall certainly advise you within a few days as to what I have found for you."

"Oh, you are very good. There —there was something else I wanted to ask you about."

"By all means, do so."

"I —I find that I want a fairly large sum of money, Mr. Green. I could easily borrow it elsewhere on the security of what I have, but I prefer to get it from you if you can arrange it."

"Ah! What is the security, Mrs. Carter?"

For answer she took a small black leather case from somewhere inside her jacket and pressed the catch. As the lid flew up she passed it over, and the Jew gasped with admiration at the superb gems which lay inside, glittering with a thousand hues.

"I have been offered fifty thousand for it by Reinhardt's, the big jewellers," she went on calmly, "but I do not care to sell it. I could easily borrow what I need from them but do not wish to."

"How much do you want?" asked Green.

"Twenty-five thousand."

"It is a lot of money, Mrs. Carter. Mind! Not that I think the necklace isn't worth that."

"I expect to pay well for the accommodation," she murmured:

"Just so. H'm. I think, perhaps, I can arrange the advance. I am not judge enough of stones to pass an opinion on the exact value of these. You won't mind my getting expert opinion, will you?"

"Not at all. You could send them around to Reinhardt's. They have, as I said, offered me fifty thousand for them."

"Thank you. I shall do so. Will you wait? It won't take long."

She murmured her assent, and excusing himself, Green rose and made his way across the office. Opening the door he disappeared through, but he was of too cautious a nature to permit anyone, be they ever so innocent, to remain alone in his office. Consequently, as soon as he had gone a clerk entered and began busily turning over a pile of papers as though he were taking advantage of the opportunity to get through some necessary work.

On reaching the outer office Green moved over to the window and examined the beautiful gems for a few moments. Then he placed them back in the case with a slow smile, and returned to his own room.

The clerk, who had been engrossed with the bundle of papers, seemed to find what he wanted at that same moment, for he abstracted a sheet from the pile and made his way out. As the door closed Green turned to his fair client.

"I found that my partner, Mr. Smart, was in, Mrs. Carter, so it was unnecessary to send the necklace to Reinhardt's. He endorses the opinion which they gave you, and, considering the fact that you will be doing all your business through us, I think I can manage to advance you the amount you require on it."

"Thank you, it is very good of you to trouble. And the interest!"

Green waved his hand.

"Oh, that will be a trifle, considering," he said suavely. "Er —for exactly how long do you wish the loan?"

"To-day is Monday. I shall return in one week to repay it. I shall also have a further twenty-five thousand with me for —er—"

"Investing," finished Green beaming. "Well, in that case, suppose we make the interest nominal, say five hundred pounds for the accommodation."

"That will be quite satisfactory."

"Will you take a cheque, or do you prefer notes?"

"Notes would be more convenient," she murmured.

"In that case it will be necessary to go round to my bankers. I shall make out a receipt here for it, and if you will come there with me, I can leave the necklace with them for safe keeping, give you the notes, and settle the matter at once."

"Thank you, that will be very nice."

22

While Green drew out a form from a pigeon-hole in his desk and filled it in, his visitor lowered her heavy black veil and sat apparently with her eyes on the floor. Had he been able to pierce the baffling web of that veil, however, he would have seen that the wide, innocent eyes were studying him from under lowered lids, and that a mocking smile was playing about the lovely lips.

He did not see these, however, and wrote on, filled with a lively satisfaction at the unexpected events of the morning. If Solomon Green had one passion in life besides the acquisition of money it was the collecting of gems, and from the moment his fat fingers had lingered caressingly over the regal stones which went to make up the scintillating necklace, he had silently vowed that before he finished with his fair client he would possess that string of gems.

When he had finished he folded the paper and stuffed it in his pocket. Then, with a murmured apology to his client, he crossed and got his immaculately brushed silk hat and picked up a gold-topped stick.

"Now, Mrs. Carter," he said, smiling his oily smile, "if you are ready."

She rose.

"My motor is waiting for me," she said. "Will you come in that?"

"I shall be most delighted," he replied, and out they went. Had Green had any doubts about the hundred and fifty thousand which the young Australian claimed to possess, they vanished immediately when he saw the luxurious motor waiting at the kerb.

From the tip of the hood to the back of the tonneau, from its rich ivory-coloured body to the deep purple upholstering, its whole appearance spoke of quiet yet expensive tastes, with the means whereby to gratify them, and the general tone of it all was in no way detracted from by the uniformed chauffeur, who sat like a carven statue, his eyes apparently fixed in their sockets.

Bowing his client in, Mr. Green sank down with a sigh of content beside her, and at her request, gave the address of his bankers — Messrs. Brice and Gibbs, Threadneedle Street.

Silently the big, high-powered car drew away from the kerb, and under the expert hand of its driver, threaded its way through several narrow streets until it stopped before the portals of Brice and Gibbs, bankers.

Five minutes later Solomon Green with his new client was seated in the private office of Mr. Brice, the senior partner, who was only too pleased to take charge of the magnificent necklace and to provide notes against Green's cheque for such a valued customer as was the Jew.

These pleasant details settled, Solomon Green and his newest client departed to part at the kerb, she once more entering the waiting motor, while he, with an expansive bow, strutted jauntily down the street, totally unconscious of the astonishing complications which were weaving themselves about him, for his fair widowed client was Mademoiselle Yvonne, who had evolved in her pretty head a remarkably simple, though effective scheme, for the despoiling of Mr. Solomon Green.

Solomon Green stared at the empty case with open-mouthed astonishment.

The Third Chapter. Mr. Brice's Temptation —One Night Only— Gone.

MR. STEPHEN BRICE, senior partner in the firm of Brice and Gibbs, bankers, leaned back in his softly padded chair and tapped his well kept teeth with the end of his pen. Of medium height, about fifty, well groomed, immaculately dressed, with pleasant eyes surmounting an aquiline nose, which fitted admirably with his well-trimmed moustache and pointed silver beard, he was an ideal type of the prosperous banker.

No man had a better name for soundness and integrity than had Stephen Brice, and, although his firm was not as large as perhaps many other institutions, it stood for safety —with a capital —and that satisfied the partners.

Possessing a marvellous capacity for work, Stephen Brice had hardly paused since he founded the banking house twenty years before. In fact, until barely a year before, he had not taken time to marry, and like so many men who remain single until that age, when the notion did occur it had its inception in the pink and white attractions of a fluffy young thing more fitted to be his daughter.

No wish of his young bride's was too much for the doting husband to fulfil, and be it said that she gave in return an honest affection. Still, when a man of fifty allows his head to be overruled by his heart, he is pretty certain to regret it, and Mr. Stephen Brice was on the point of doing something which was going to cause him an ocean of remorse.

As he sat abstractedly tapping his teeth, his common-sense said "No!" and he declared most emphatically that the thing was harmless —yes —but most irregular —most nonsensical, and he would not do it —no, not even for Ethel, his wife. On the other hand his heart said "Yes!" and between the two he hesitated.

Then, rising, he walked across to the big vault, swung open the door, took from a shelf within a small leather case sealed with the firm's seal, and walking back to his desk, sat down and contemplated the case with dubious eyes.

It was then that his common-sense heaved a sigh of regret and flew away while his heart leaped up victorious. He had hesitated and was lost. The decision which he had found it so difficult to make had arisen from his graphic description to his wife of the beautiful

25

diamond necklace which he had received into his care.

So realistic had it been, that nothing would do but she must see it. Acquiescing as usual, he had shown it to her the previous day, and that night she had pleaded, with appealing eyes, to be allowed to wear it to the Opera the following night.

That was on Wednesday, and now, on this Thursday, he sat debating the point. Of course, it could do no harm to let her wear it just that one night. Of course, if she had been going without him, he would never have considered it for a moment, but he would be with her every moment.

True, he had never done a similar thing since he had been a banker. Never had a seal been broken on a package once it had been placed in the vault. Already the seal on the black jewel-case had been broken and freshly sealed when he returned it to the shelf, after showing it to his wife.

Almost unconsciously, while he was pondering, he broke the seal again and pressed the catch. Up flew the lid, and as soon as his eyes rested on the perfect gems he was definitely lost.

"How lovely they had looked when Ethel placed them about her throat yesterday!" he muttered. "Just to-night. To-morrow I can return them first thing. Yes, I'll do it —for her."

With a quick, almost an ashamed motion, he picked up the necklace and stuffed it in his pocket. Then, closing the case, he once more sealed it and returned it to the vault. Slamming the heavy steel door, he set the time lock, and got ready to depart.

Ten minutes later he ran down the steps with the light step and anticipatory smile of a boy. Ethel would be happy, and nothing else mattered.

And she was happy. Nor were his nervous fears realised then. They duly went to the Opera, and he glowed with happiness as he contemplated the lovely picture his girl-wife made. She had donned a gown of unrelieved black, which made her white shoulders look like alabaster. Against the throat of ivory gleamed the splendid gems, and truly she was a fitting target for the many glasses which were turned on her that night.

Over in a box, on the other side of the house, sat Solomon Green with his overdressed wife. He made it a point to subscribe at the beginning of the season, and with his wife was a regular attendant.

Not that he knew anything about music. He couldn't have told the difference between the Ninth Symphony and the nine hundredth rag-time. It pleased him, however, to see his name in the list of subscribers under that of Lord So-and-So, and whatever capital accrued therefrom, be sure he made the most of it.

Like many others in the house that night, he turned his glasses on the radiant young creature in the box across from him, and with a quick start he recognised the necklace which she wore. He was too keen a judge to be mistaken on that score.

His statement, to his fair client, that the presence of his partner Smart had made it unnecessary to send the necklace to Reinhardt's had been a lie, for no such man as Smart existed. He had merely desired a few moments alone in order to assure himself that the stones were all they seemed, and on his own judgment had advanced the loan.

"So," he muttered, "Brice is beginning that kind of thing, eh! I think I shall lose no time in shifting my account. Truly, there is no fool like an old fool; and when a banker borrows gems, which have been left in his keeping, in order to please his wife, it's not good enough for Solomon Green. I wouldn't have done that for Sarah. He'll be borrowing the money next. Solomon, my boy, you must shift that account."

The next morning when Stephen Brice reached his office he heaved a sigh of relief. The first thing he did was to open the vault and take out the black jewel-case. Then, replacing the necklace, he closed it, and once more carefully sealed it.

That done he put it back in the vault, and went about his day's work, glad that his wife had been pleased, but gladder still that the gems were back in the vault all right.

Punctually at ten o'clock the following Monday morning Mr. Solomon Green reached Threadneedle Street, and entered the banking premises of Brice & Gibbs. He was ushered in at once to the senior partner, and after a few moments' conversation, Stephen Brice went to the vault and got the black jewel-case.

As yet Green had said nothing regarding the withdrawal of his account, nor did he intend to until the end of the month. He resolved to do so then, and should Brice ask the reason, he had made up his mind to tell him. Consequently, he was as oily as ever, and after a few more banalities, during which he examined the seal, he tucked the case in his capacious inside pocket, and took his departure.

Going by the nearest way, he made his own offices in ten minutes, and passed into his private room at exactly half-past ten. A clerk was busy turning over papers in the eternal pile, which seemed to interest him on certain occasions; and, sitting in the same seat she had occupied a week previously, was the young widow who had resolved to place her burdens on the expansive shoulders of Mr. Solomon Green.

He smiled and greeted her effusively.

"Good-morning, Mrs. Carter," he said, shaking hands. "Unlike most of my feminine clients, you are prompt to the minute."

"I knew how busy you were," she murmured in reply, as she threw back her veil, once more causing Green's thoughts to dwell on Romano's and supper.

"I brought the money in order to repay the loan, and besides that, I brought an extra twenty-five thousand."

"Ah! that is very satisfactory," replied Green, rubbing his hands together. "I have just been to the bank for the case. Here it is."

He drew it out and laid it on the desk for her.

"I suppose I ought to examine the seal?" she said with a faint smile.

"Ha, ha!" he laughed, with all the mirth born of the thought of that second twenty-five thousand, which she said she had brought. "You are learning already, Mrs. Carter. Caution is the first point in business. By all means examine it."

Picking it up, she turned the case about and looked at the seal, then with another smile handed it back.

"It seems all right, Mr. Green. I am afraid I wouldn't know whether it was or not."

Nor did Green dream, for the millionth part of a second, that those few moments, during which the case had rested in her hands, were to cost him every penny that he had advanced on the necklace.

At that moment the clerk, who had retired, entered and laid some letters on Green's desk, just as the latter broke the seal on the case. The young widow was busy counting over a pile of crisp notes which she had taken from her purse, and both she and Green suspended operations until the clerk had withdrawn.

Then, after a furtive look at the notes, Solomon Green pressed the catch, and the lid flew up; but as he looked, the oily smile froze on his face, his fat body trembled as with the ague, the cold sweat stood out in great beads on his forehead, and his hand shook like an aspen.

The necklace was gone!

"My heavens!" he gasped, too utterly stupefied to say more.

"What is it?" cried his client, starting up in apparent agitation.

Green turned the case around and showed her the empty interior. Then he drew it back, and with laboured breathing bent over it. His horrified gaze and his fat, shaking fingers examined every inch of the interior, as though he expected to find the heap of stones hidden behind a minute bulge in the white lining.

Then, with the despairing air of a drowning man, he turned the case over and over, end for end, upside down. He pounded it, he hammered it on the table, he clawed at it, but his poundings brought only a dull, empty echo; his hammerings only dented the corners, and his clawing but soiled the lining.

"My heavens! My heavens! My heavens!" he sang out in despair. "Gone! Mrs. Carter, gone!"

"It seems so," replied his client coldly, as she picked up the case and made pretence of examining it.

Her tones brought Green's agitation under control as nothing else could have done. With a snap of the jaw he sat up and reached out for the case. Once more he critically examined it. Somehow, somewhere, something had happened to abstract the necklace from the case. He had received it from Brice, had walked straight to his office, and had not broken the seal until he did so before his client. Then, like lightning, his mind went back to the previous Thursday night at the Opera, and he remembered what he had seen.

"Mrs. Carter," he said thickly, "there is some mistake somewhere. I won't say more at present. The necklace is all right, you needn't fear for that. I swear to you I haven't even seen the case, much less touched it since you and I both saw Mr. Brice seal it and put it in the vault. I went for it at ten o'clock this morning and came direct here. You yourself examined the bank's seal before I broke it. I am very glad now that you did. It seems to be the same case, but perhaps Brice has given me another one by mistake, or —" but he did not voice the thought.

"That is hardly possible," she replied, gathering up her notes and thrusting them back in her purse. "The case was made specially for the necklace, and I know it too well to be mistaken. It is my case, no other. A week ago to-day I came here, Mr. Green, and handed you my necklace. You loaned me twenty-five thousand pounds on it, and in accordance with my promise I came back to-day with fifty thousand —fifty thousand five hundred to be exact. I accept your statement that you have not touched the necklace since that day, but I have come for it, and I want it, please."

"Yes, yes!" cried the bewildered Green. "You shall have it. Yes, yes; all right —all right. Yes, yes!" he stuttered on.

"It seems to me," went on his client, "that you had better phone the bank. I know that the seal was all right when you brought the case here. I do not know what kind of a firm Brice & Gibbs is, but the necklace is not visible in the case, and as you seem to know nothing about it, there is no time to be lost in making inquiries there."

Almost before she had finished speaking, Green had lifted down the receiver, and was putting through a call for Brice & Gibbs.

To the agitated Jew, it seemed an age before one of the bank's clerks had answered, and an eternity before he heard Brice's voice.

"Is that you, Brice?" he almost shouted. "Did you make a mistake in the case you gave me? You didn't? What's wrong? This is wrong. The necklace is not in it! Are you there? Hello, hello! Are you there?"

In his impatience, Green worked the hook up and down repeatedly, the while he shouted his futile question to a dead wire, for at the other end Stephen Brice reeled back from the instrument, and quietly fell forward, sprawled over his desk in a dead faint.

The Jew went purple with impatience and anxiety, and shouted himself hoarse, unheeding of the presence of his client. Still that unresponsive, irritating silence met him; then came a faint buzzing, followed by a click, and he knew someone had hung up the receiver.

"My heavens'" he panted, turning his head. "I'll have to go round to the bank at once, Mrs. Carter. I don't know what has happened, but you needn't worry about the necklace. It will be all right."

"I am glad to hear you say so, Mr. Green. I will go with you and wait outside until you bring it."

The Jew nodded and, rising heavily, got his hat. Then, picking up the black jewel-case, he glanced inquiringly at his client.

"Are you ready, Mrs. Carter?" he asked, still speaking as one labouring under the stress of a great emotion.

"Quite," she replied rising. "Don't you think it would be as well as to take the cord and broken seal which secured the case?" she added, pointing to them where they lay on the desk.

"Yes, I had forgotten. It would be better."

Green picked them up, and led the way to the door. Then, preceded by the other, he followed her out to the street, where the imposing car panted at the kerb as it had exactly a week before. And as Green sank into the embrace of the soft cushions, how different were his feelings from those of the previous Monday!

Then he had been in the first flush of his success over the promotion of the Golden Princess Mine. On top of that had come the charming young widow with plenty of money and a dearth of experience. All the week he had dwelt on the pleasurable anticipation of investing her funds for her in such a way that they would eventually rest secure in his pockets.

After that he was determined that once more he would get the necklace in his hands. She would certainly need money, and when that time arrived would be unable to redeem it. Then he would be magnanimous to a certain extent.

Indeed, he had gone so far as to ponder on the advisability of keeping the Golden Princess Mine afloat a little longer. That would give him a ready-made investment at his hand, and she would never know the difference.

Now, however, all his plans had come tumbling about his ears like a pack of cards. To make matters worse, she had turned up punctually with the money to redeem the necklace, and twenty-five thousand besides. He didn't propose letting that slip through his fingers if he could help it, but as yet he was too bewildered over the sudden disappearance of the contents of the case to evolve a new plan.

He never dreamed for a moment but that he would get the gems on his arrival at the bank. True, he could swear he had seen them on Brice's wife at the Opera, but the banker wouldn't dare try to bluff him off with the sealed case in an empty condition, even if he had succumbed to temptation. No, such a thing was unthinkable, though Green, a crook himself, was ready to believe evil of any fellow-man.

As the car rolled silently along, he went over in his mind every movement of the case from the time he had passed it over to Brice & Gibbs. The only circumstance on which he could build any explanation was the fact that Brice had borrowed the necklace on one occasion. Therein, the Jew felt he would find the reason for the empty case, and the feeling did not decrease his anger against Brice.

Innocent as was his new client, she might get suspicious over the occurrence, and once in possession of the necklace again, decide that she would invest through a different channel. That she had anything to do with the disappearance of the necklace never entered Green's mind.

At the entrance to the banking premises of Brice & Gibbs the car pulled up, and Green turned inquiringly to his companion.

"Will you wait here as you said, Mrs. Carter, or would you prefer to come in?"

"Oh, I'll wait here. You won't be long, will you?"

"No, indeed —just long enough to get the necklace and receive an explanation of how the mistake occurred."

She nodded.

"Then I won't bother to go in."

Green rose to get out, then turned to pick up the black jewel-case which had lain on the seat between them. His client already had it in her hand, however, and nodded at him.

"I'll pass it to you after you get out," she said.

The Jew again turned and, with the slow heaviness of movement peculiar to him, stepped out of the car.

The moment his back was turned his fair client did a most peculiar thing for one of her apparent ignorance of the world and its ways. Holding the case with one hand, she whipped up the end of the purple cushion where Green had been sitting. Thrusting the case under, she grasped something else.

When her hand emerged it was again holding a black jewel-case identical in shape, size, and colour with the other. Indeed, so rapid were her movements that the closest observer would have found it difficult to believe she was not holding the same case. Pushing the cushion back into place, she barely had time to assume her former attitude when Green turned round and reached up for the case.

Not for a moment did he think it was other than the one which had lain under his hand during the journey from his office. Something in the cool composure of the woman must have served to steady his own nerves, for when he lifted his hat and started across the pavement it was with nearly all his old jauntiness of manner.

As soon as he had disappeared through the swing doors of the bank Yvonne leaned forward and spoke in low tones to the chauffeur. In a moment the big motor was beginning to move, rapidly it gathered speed, and threading through the traffic disappeared from view, just as the slim, veiled girl in the back pressed a button set in the side, causing the number at the back to change with remarkable rapidity.

All unconscious of the departure of the car, Solomon Green was making his way to the private office of Stephen Brice. What had occurred to break the connection while he had been speaking on the 'phone he had no idea, but as soon as he entered it became plain.

Brice was leaning back in his chair, looking white and shaken. Gibbs, his partner, a younger man, thin, clean-shaven, and wearing glasses, was hanging over him solicitously. On the desk before him was a glass half full of water, and a small square of paper showed that Brice had just taken a powder.

He gazed dully at Green as the latter pushed his way into the office, and Gibbs turned irritably, for Brice had not told his partner the reason of his fainting spell.

"I'm afraid you will have to wait a few minutes, Mr. Green." said Gibbs brusquely. "Mr. Brice is unwell. Would you mind sitting in the outside office until he feels better?"

For answer, Green closed the door and turned the key. The fact that his remark on the 'phone had affected Brice so seriously, and the knowledge that he had not told his partner the reason of his seizure, had roused once more all the Jew's suspicious nature. For a moment a cold hand seemed to rest on his heart, for he knew his own position to be decidedly unenviable were his fair client to insist upon the return of her necklace at once.

"I guess he'll talk to me now," he said thickly. "And you, too," he added. "At any rate, I can tell you this —I don't unlock that door until I know what has become of the necklace."

"The necklace!" echoed the bewildered Gibbs, gazing at Green as though that gentleman had suddenly taken leave of his senses. "I don't understand you. What is it you mean?"

"Look at your partner," sneered Green. "Ask him." With that he walked to the desk and slammed down the case. Then he tossed the cord on top of it and pointed an accusing finger at Brice.

"Now then," he demanded, "where is it?"

Gibbs was gazing at his partner in dismay. What had happened he knew not, but that it was something serious he began to gather from Green's manner. Finally, Brice lifted his haggard face and looked at Green.

"The necklace was in the case and the seal unbroken when I

handed it to you this morning," he said hoarsely.

"Oh, was it? Then tell me how it disappeared," snapped Green. "I took the case from you and went direct to my office. I didn't break the seal until I got there, and then only when it had been examined by the owner. In addition to that, a clerk of mine was in the office at the time, so I have two witnesses to swear that the necklace was not in the case. What have you to say?"

"See here —what is this all about?" interrupted Gibbs, staring in amazement from his partner to Green.

"He left that case here for safe keeping a week ago," answered Brice. "I delivered it to him this morning, and a few moments after he reached his office he telephoned that the gems were not in the case."

"And of course you can swear they were?" exclaimed Gibbs, glaring at Green.

Brice lifted his hand and let it fall again.

"Yes," he said slowly. "Yes, I can swear they were in the case."

Green bent forward and leaned his hands on the desk.

"Will you swear that the case has been untouched ever since I left it here?" he asked harshly.

Brice gave a choking gasp and essayed to speak. His partner stood gazing at him with a dawning anxiety, and was about to answer the question himself when Green interrupted.

"And will you swear that your wife didn't wear that necklace at the Opera last Thursday night?" he demanded remorselessly.

Brice stared at him with fascinated gaze, but made no reply.

"But, of course, this is all nonsense!" ejaculated Gibbs, looking at his partner for confirmation of the fact. At last speech came to Stephen Brice, and he sat up.

"No, it is true," he said. "I did take the necklace on Thursday, and my wife did wear it that night. I returned it to the cage on Friday morning, however. That I swear on my honour! From that moment until I handed it back this morning, it has been untouched and the seal unbroken. If it has disappeared, it has been since it left here."

"A likely story!" sneered Green hotly. "I tell you that there was no necklace in the case when I opened it, and I can prove my statement. I left it here for safe keeping, and this is how you fulfil your trust. I want it, and I want it at once! If I don't get it, I'll appeal to the law. You know what that will mean. Come, are you going to wreck your business for the sake of keeping the necklace? You know as well as I do that the moment such a thing becomes public you won't keep a customer. Pass it back, and beyond withdrawing my account I'll say nothing. If not, I swear I'll take action at once. My client demands it of me, and I demand it of you!"

"I swear to you that I have not got the necklace," cried Brice hoarsely. "It is true I took it for Thursday evening, but that is all. It was a mistake —yes, but I returned it."

"You made no mistake about the case, I suppose?" broke in Gibbs, turning towards the vault.

Brice shook his head.

"No, that is impossible. There was no other case of similar appearance. Are you sure it isn't in the case?" he added desperately to Green.

For answer the latter jerked the article in question across the desk, and pressed the catch.

"See for yourself," he exclaimed savagely. "I— Good heavens! What is this?"

He, as well as Brice, stared in stupefaction at the contents, and Gibbs, reading the alarm in his tones, turned back from the vault and hastened across. There, where the necklace ought to have been, was a neat pile of gilt-edged share certificates, and Solomon Green needed no second look to tell him that they were certificates of the Golden Princess Mining Company.

With blanched cheeks, he put out a shaking hand and lifted them out. Then he abstracted one from the bundle and opened it. It was, as he thought, a share certificate in the mine, and a sudden thought crossed his mind as he saw it was filled in to the Honourable Algernon Montague Bayes. Again that cold hand seemed clutching at his heart.

Slowly he turned the certificate over, and saw in one glance that it had been assigned to one "Mary Jones."

In that moment Solomon Green knew he had been done, but how it had happened he could not imagine. It had been an utter mystery how the necklace had disappeared, but that he had put down to Brice. Now the case, which he could have sworn was empty when he left his office, contained a pile of share certificates.

It needed all his self-control to master the inclination of his mind just then. He knew, however, if he betrayed his knowledge it would break the strength of his chances of recovering from the bankers. So, collecting his wits, and folding up the certificate, he replaced it in the bundle and thrust them in his pocket.

"It shows how shocked I was at discovering the disappearance of the necklace," he said coolly. "These certificates were on my desk, and before coming I put them in the case instead of in my pocket. There is the case, and as you can see for yourself it is empty. Here is the cord, and you can still see bits of the seal sticking to it. Now, then, you know how much I loaned on the stones, for you cashed my cheque, and saw me hand the notes to my client."

Brice nodded.

"Yes—twenty-five thousand."

"Then you know the necklace was worth double that, and if you doubt it my statement can be proved by Reinhardt's, the jewellers. I make a final demand. Will you return me that necklace, or must I take action?"

"I tell you it was in that case when you took it this morning," blazed Brice.

"Wait!" broke in Gibbs, holding up his hand. "It is now past eleven, Mr. Green. Give us until three o'clock this afternoon. If we cannot locate the necklace by then we will communicate with you at once."

And Green, because he was madly anxious to reach his office and think over the startling events, agreed. He reached for the case, but Gibbs was before him, and, without apparently noticing the Jew's intention, carried it across and placed it in the vault. Then he unlocked the door.

"Three o'clock, Mr. Green," he said significantly.

The promoter nodded, turned as though to speak, evidently thought better of it, and departed. He could hardly keep his feet from breaking into a run as he passed through the outer office, for a sudden fear had assailed him—a fear that somebody somewhere was working against him, and the very mystery of the affair had caused his mind to suspect everybody and everything.

He ran down the steps and crossed the kerb, not noticing in his absorption that the grey car was not there. As he lifted his head to address his client, however, he gasped aloud. It was gone, and with it the last bit of solid ground in the matter.

Had she grown tired of waiting, and would he find her at his office? Or was she less ignorant than she appeared, and was she mixed up in the mystery which was enveloping him? Why had she left? Where had she gone? These and a dozen other questions raced through his mind as he stood there gazing up and down the street.

Then, with a silent curse, he turned and began walking quickly, intent on reaching his office. There he felt he could evolve something out of the chaos of events, and arrange his movements in order to ensure that if anybody was to lose over the disappearance of the necklace it would not be Solomon Green.

'The bank-manager dropped forward in a faint as the voice of Solomon Green came along the wire: "The necklace—it is gone!"

SEXTON BLAKE leisurely ascended the steps of the banking premises of Brice & Gibbs, pushed his way through the swing doors, and strode along past the neatly-labelled cages until he reached the inquiry desk at the far end. The moment he gave his name, the clerk to whom he spoke left his seat and ushered him into the private office of Stephen Brice.

It was barely an hour since Solomon Green had departed after delivering his ultimatum. The two partners sat on opposite sides of Brice'e desk, the opened jewel-case and fragment of cord testifying to the fact that the astounding disappearance of the necklace had been under constant discussion. Brice still looked haggard and worried, and, though Gibbs had an anxious gleam in his eye, his jaw was set with the determination to ferret the thing out at all costs.

With that end in view he had requested Green to give them until three o'clock, and as soon as the promoter had gone he got on the 'phone to Sexton Blake. The younger partner had heard all Brice could tell him, and, while admitting the grave mistake of borrowing the gems for an evening, he felt absolutely convinced of the integrity of his senior.

As clerk, teller, accountant, cashier, and finally junior partner he had worked with the other. In the years which had passed he had grown to realise that Stephen Brice was a man of the highest honour, and, had he wished to possess a necklace for his wife, his financial resources would have stood the strain. It was unthinkable that he had suddenly developed a criminal streak; and on his own knowledge of the man Gibbs accepted the statement that the necklace had duly been returned to its case on the morning after the Opera.

There was no getting away from the fact that it had disappeared, however. If he felt the sincerity of his partner's words, he felt equally sure that Green had not had anything to do with its abstraction from the jewel-case.

He knew Green for what he was, but the very fact that he knew so much about the promoter forbade the theory that he had taken the gems. Solomon Green would never be so crude as to try a bluff like that, nor would he do anything of such a risky nature. No! Whichever way the anxious junior partner looked at it he got lost in a maze, and when Blake entered he looked up with an expression of relief.

After greeting the partners Blake drew up a chair and deposited his silk hat on the floor. At a single glance he had seen the open jewel-case and the cord. The same glance had confirmed his reading of the urgent tones over the 'phone, when he had been asked to come at once. He made no reference to these things, however, but turned to the senior partner.

"Now, Mr. Brice," he said briskly, "if you will be good enough to state the matter on which you wish my advice I shall be obliged."

Brice waved his hand to Gibbs.

"Tell Mr. Blake," he said. "I'll answer any questions afterwards."

Gibbs nodded, and turned to the detective.

"I'll state the case as briefly as possible, Mr. Blake. You see that empty black jewel-case on the desk?"

Blake nodded, though he seemed to be gazing vacantly through the window.

"A week ago this morning," went on Gibbs, "a customer of ours brought that case here and left it with Mr. Brice for safe keeping. It contained a diamond necklace of great value on which the customer in question had loaned a large sum— twenty-five thousand pounds, to be exact. He had loaned it to a client—a woman —who came with him and received the notes here. Then they departed, and until Wednesday nothing occurred which would have any bearing on the matter. On that day, however, my partner's wife was here, and after hearing Mr. Brice's description of the stones begged to see it. He took it from the vault and showed it to her. Then he sealed it and put it back.

"That night his wife pleaded to be allowed to wear it just for one evening —to the Opera on Thursday. At first he refused, realising that, though it would probably be safe enough, it was irregular. However, after thinking the matter over, he gave in, and when he left on Thursday took the necklace home with him.

"That evening Mrs. Brice wore it to the Opera, and it happened that in a box across from them was the customer who had left it here for safe keeping. We now know that he recognised it.

"The next morning it was returned to its case, and after that had been again sealed it was placed back in the vault. Nothing else happened until this morning at a little past ten o'clock. Then the customer who had left it arrived and asked for it.

"My partner handed it over, and after noting that the seal was all right the customer departed. Shortly after my partner received a telephone message saying that when he opened the case the necklace was not there. The news upset Mr. Brice, and he fainted. A clerk called me, and I came in at once.

"While I was looking after him, the customer arrived bringing the empty case and cord which you see on the desk. He swears that the case was empty when he opened it, and says he can produce two witnesses —his client and a clerk —who can prove what he says. He then demanded the immediate production of the necklace by my partner, and—well, to be frank, intimated that Mr. Brice had stolen it. He mentioned the fact that he had seen it on Mrs. Brice at the Opera, and I presume based his accusation on that.

"I asked him to stave off his client's demands and give us until three o'clock to produce it. You can readily see, Mr. Blake, that unless we can hand it over we face ruin. He threatens that, unless we do so, he will expose the matter, and you know what even the barest rumour of that kind will do for a bank. We should be pushed to the wall in twenty-four hours."

"A thing which your customer realises and is taking advantage of," commented Blake drily. "However, there are a few questions I wish to ask, Mr. Gibbs."

"I am at your service. Mr. Blake."

Blake turned to Brice.

"Mr. Gibbs related all the facts as you both know them, I presume?" he asked bluntly.

The senior partner nodded, "Yes, every point."

"And I suppose you would not have sought my assistance if it had been true that you took them?" continued the detective.

"Mr. Brice has passed his word of honour that the case is exactly as I stated it," broke in Gibbs. "I accept that, and am willing to pledge my life that you can also, Mr. Blake."

"That's all right, then. In a matter of this kind I want to know exactly where I stand. Now then, a few questions. Firstly, what is the name of the customer who left the necklace here for safe keeping?"

"I thought you would ask that. His name is Green —Solomon Green."

"Of Green & Smart?"

"Yes."

"I understood you to say that the seal was unbroken when the case left here this morning?"

"Yes."

"Have you any reason to suppose that he would take advantage of the fact that Mrs. Brice wore the necklace to the Opera in order to retain it himself and use that fact as a weapon of blackmail?"

"That was the first thought which crossed my mind, Mr. Blake. I think it very improbable that Solomon Green would attempt anything so risky. Besides, his agitation over the loss was too genuine."

"Do you know the name of his client who owns it?"

"I heard him call her Mrs. Carter," put in Brice. "I never saw her before. She was young, and I should think from the manner in which she was dressed, a wealthy young widow."

"From what I know of your customer, Mr. Green, quite the usual type of client he aims at," remarked Blake thoughtfully, "I suppose, Mr. Brice you are sure nobody could tamper with the case from the time you returned the necklace to it until you gave it to Solomon Green this morning?"

"No one. Of that I am certain."

"Then, supposing it was still in the case this morning, it seems evident that it disappeared between the time Green left here and his telephone call telling you it was missing. By the way who did he say could prove the case was empty when he opened it in his office?"

"His client and a clerk," relied Gibbs.

"It is fairly safe to assume that his clerk would swear to whatever his employer told him to?" said Blake. "However, that is a point for consideration. Another point is his client. I must know whether she was quite all she seemed. Although you seem to eliminate Green from any hanky-panky business, he is one of the few human figures in the matter which must be investigated. Now I should like to examine the case."

Brice lifted it up and passed it across.

Blake, after scrutinising the outside carefully, carried it across to the window and held it so that the light fell on the inside. Then, after noting that it contained no maker's name, he drew out the powerful pocket-glass and began studying each portion of the white-satin lining. That finished, he closed the cover and laid the case on the window-sill.

Then, dropping to his knees, he again brought the glass into requisition, and went over the black leather covering, paying particular attention to the meeting-place of top and bottom.

It was impossible to tell from his expression whether his examination had yielded anything or not, for, on rising, he carelessly tossed the case back on the desk and picked up the cord. Once more he went to the window and devoted the same attention to the cord and broken seal which he had given to the case.

After several minutes, during which the partners eyed him anxiously, he turned and resumed his seat.

"Where did you tie and seal the case?" he asked abruptly, turning to Brice.

"Why —er —right here on the desk."

"Were you sitting where you are now?"

"Yes."

"Do you think you could repeat the action in detail?"

"Oh, I think so!"

"Remember it would be of no benefit unless you could."

"Well, I tie up and seal thousands of packages in the course of a year —banknotes, jewels, and the like. My method is invariably the same. I always use the same kind of cord, the same sealing-wax, and stamp it with the seal of the bank."

"Do you always tie the same kind of knot?"

"Naturally! That is a habit."

"Very well, Mr. Brice. Please take that case and a new piece of string. Tie it up and seal it exactly as you did before."

With a wondering look on his face Brice opened his mouth to speak, but a gesture of his partner kept him silent, and he turned to obey. Opening a drawer in the desk he took out a ball of cord of exactly the same kind as the piece lying on the desk. His practised gaze in judging the length showed him to be familiar with the work, as he had said.

After cutting off the length he had selected, he drew the case towards him, and, with the rapidity and accuracy of long habit, soon had the box tied up. Then he reached for a stick of violet sealing wax, and, unlocking a small private compartment, brought out a heavy brass seal. From another drawer he took a small piece of paper about three inches square, and slipping this under the knot, lighted a match.

For a moment Blake made a movement as though to speak, but evidently altered his mind, for he sank back again and watched in silence.

Brice lighted a match, and holding it near the end of the stick of sealing-wax, guided the melting drops on to the knot. When a fair amount had covered the knot, and run over on to the slip of paper underneath, he gave the stick a rapid twirl in order to prevent any more wax from dropping, and, laying it on the blotting-pad, pressed the brass seal heavily on the wax-covered knot.

"I presume that slip of paper is to prevent any wax from getting on the case and disfiguring it," remarked Blake, as Brice finished and looked up.

"Oh, yes! Sometimes I wrap the package in paper first, but not always."

"I see. Will you now undo what you have done, please?"

The banker looked a trifle annoyed, as though he thought Blake was putting him through a useless pantomime, but began at once to break the seal and remove the cord.

As for Gibbs, he sat in gloomy silence, alternately watching his partner and the detective.

When the case was once more free of the cord, Blake picked it up and walked again to the window. There he applied the glass to his eye, and went over every inch of the soft padded leather covering. As he finished, his jaw stiffened a trifle, but was still non-committal.

"I suppose you are prepared to swear this is the same case which you received originally?" he said slowly, as he sat down.

"Good heavens—yes!" exclaimed Brice. "I am positive."

"Counting the present occasion, you have tied it and sealed it four separate times altogether, haven't you?"

"Yes; when Green first brought it, on Wednesday when I opened it to show it to my wife, on Friday when I returned it after she had worn it at the Opera, and just now."

"Exactly. I suppose you tied the cord as firmly as on the present occasion?"

"Certainly. More so, if anything."

"And you can think of no other detail which you may have neglected to tell me?"

"One little thing happened which seemed rather queer at the time," remarked Gibbs.

"What was it?"

"Well, after Green 'phoned that he couldn't find the necklace in the case, he came right on here, as you know. We discussed the thing for a few moments before he opened the case. When he did so, however, it was filled with a bundle of share certificates, and at first he seemed awfully surprised. We were too much upset at the time to pay much attention to the incident, but now that I have had time to think things over, it strikes me as peculiar."

"Did he say anything?"

"He opened one of the certificates, read it, and then thrust the whole lot into his pocket. Said he was under the impression he had put them there before coming here, but must have been so excited he stuck them in the case unthinkingly."

For a full moment Blake sat motionless. Then he reached out his hand and picked up the case and the piece of cord which had been around it in the morning.

"Well, gentlemen," he said, as he put them in his pocket, "the matter certainly presents several knotty points. I cannot pass any opinion at present. One or two ideas have occurred to me, but they must receive some thought. It is now almost one o'clock. I shall devote the rest of the day to the affair, and perhaps by to-morrow may be in a position to make a definite move."

"But we have only got until three o'clock," gasped Brice and Gibbs together.

"I intend that Mr. Solomon Green shall do nothing for the present." replied Blake coolly, "Before I go, I want you to ring him up on the 'phone."

"Do you wish to speak with him?" asked Brice.

"No. I want you to do the talking. This is what you are to say. Tell him that the most careful search has failed to reveal the whereabouts of the necklace, and say that you are advising him now, as it would do no good to delay your answer until three. Then ask him if he will accept a cash settlement instead."

"But —but that is irregular," protested Brice.

"Possibly it is," replied Blake coldly. "If you wish this matter cleared up, Mr. Brice, you must please do as I ask."

Without another word the banker turned and drew the 'phone towards him. A moment later he was asking for Green & Smart's number, and the listening men heard him get into conversation with Green. When he had finished, he hung up the receiver and wiped the cold sweat from his forehead.

"I judge from what you said that he named a cash settlement," remarked Blake.

Brice nodded.

"Yes; fifty thousand. He says if we pay that, his client will be satisfied, and he will say nothing. I suppose we shall have to pay."

"You will do nothing of the sort." said Blake, rising. "All I want you both to do is —nothing. If I am to settle matters I must have everything left in my hands. I am going now to call on Mr. Green."

"I agree with what you say," exclaimed Gibbs, rising also. "I think both of us are all at sea regarding Mr. Blake's reasons, Stephen," he added, turning to his partner, "but it seems to me that our only course is to meet his wishes."

"I'll do anything," groaned Brice. "If Green lets this get out it means ruin."

Blake held out his hand.

"I don't think he will do anything for the present, after I have seen him," he smiled. "I'll let you know as soon as possible what I find."

With that he turned and made his way out, more puzzled than he cared to acknowledge.

Blake chose to walk from Threadneedle Street for the purpose of adjusting his ideas on the matter in hand, and to endeavour to allocate to their proper position several facts which might, or might not, be of an important nature.

Taking the case on its merits, and allowing for any minor faults in the relation of the facts, it seemed at first glance that either Brice or Green must be lying. To begin with, the black jewel-case had been in the hands of just three persons from the time it had been passed on to Brice on the previous Monday morning. Those persons were Solomon Green, his client, and the banker himself. By all the laws of mathematics, one of those three must be the thief.

Taking that as a working hypothesis, which one of the three would have sufficient motive? From what he knew of Solomon Green, it seemed unlikely that the promoter would risk such a thing. Not from any moral consideration, but from his desire to ensure the safety of the said Solomon Green.

On the other hand, he claimed to have both his client and a clerk to witness that he had not broken the seal before arriving at his office. That point had already been marked for investigation. Of course, if Green had got into financial difficulties he might plan and carry out such a dangerous theft, but it didn't seem compatible with the man's nature.

Then there was Brice. On the partner's own statement, Brice had no motive for doing such a thing. He had a reputation for soundness and integrity, and if ever a man was honest in his protestations, that man was Brice. Still, the fact remained that he had foolishly tampered with property left in his keeping, and though to Blake that meant nothing, it would be of a damning nature before the world at large.

Finally, there arose for consideration Green's client. Who was she and what was she? What motive would she have in stealing her own property, and, besides, supposing that she had, when could she have managed to do so? Unless she and Green were in collusion, it seemed impossible, and yet one of the three was guilty. Of this Blake felt certain.

Moreover, his examination of the case had not been as barren of result as his enigmatical expression had led the partners to believe. His first scrutiny of the black jewel-case had shown nothing, it is true, but the very fact that it did show nothing had caused him to think.

If Brice's statement was correct, it had been tied and sealed by him three times. Why, then, was it so flawless? The leather was of the finest and softest morocco, and it was unthinkable that it could stand several handlings of that description without the delicate leather showing the faintest trace when examined under the glass.

Then he had asked Brice to tie it up and seal it in a manner similar to before. On the second examination the leather had distinctly revealed marks caused by the cord, particularly where it had pressed on the edges. Why did the fourth tying reveal these, when the three previous ones had left it flawless? It was not possible for every particle of the leather to escape marking. Therefore, there was only one explanation.

The case which now reposed in his pocket was not the case which Brice had handed to Solomon Green in the morning. With that thought Blake drew a deep breath.

"That eliminates Brice," he muttered. "Therefore, the problem contains two human elements only —Green and his client. Certainly a visit to Green seems the next logical step in the proposition. What puzzles me is his offer to accept a cash settlement instead of the necklace. That might mean two or three different things.

"For instance, if he and the woman are working as confederates, and one of them has succeeded in getting the necklace, then his offer to settle degenerates into simple blackmail. He knows that Brice daren't risk exposure. It would mean the ruin of his credit.

"Again, supposing Green to be innocent of the theft, and allowing that in some way the woman has regained possession of the stones, it would mean that Green realises now that he has been done out of the twenty-five thousand which he loaned on it. In that case he would be thoroughly capable of taking advantage of Brice & Gibbs' position to play the thing for all it was worth. Hence his demand for fifty thousand on the plea that it is the value of the lost necklace. Whether he demanded half that amount or double he knows perfectly well that the bankers would be compelled to pay it to save their face.

"If that should happen to be the case, I can see where I get an opportunity of squeezing you, Mr. Solomon Green. Such a settlement would not only give him back the money he loaned on the necklace, but pay him a profit of a like amount. And that is not unlike the kind of thing which appeals to that gentleman. But here are his offices. I'll have a little chat with him, and see what he has to say."

Blake stopped long enough to send an urgent telegram to Tinker, then, tossing away his cigar, made his way into the offices of Green & Smart, every one of his brilliant faculties on the alert.

Yvonne visits the oily Solomon Green.

Mrs. Brice wears Yvonne's
necklace at the Opera.

Solomon Green plays
a waiting game.

48

EVEN as he stood in the office of Brice & Gibbs, dumbfounded at the sight of the share certificates, did Solomon Green realise that a cleverer individual than he had been using him as a mere puppet. The sight of the Honourable Algernon Montague Bayes' name on the certificate had at once sent his mind dancing back to the letter he had received from that gentleman just a week ago.

During the week he had written for the name and address of the person to whom the shares had been assigned, and only that morning had he received the Honourable Algy's reply saying he had sold them to one Mary Jones, whose address he had as 64a, Exeter Street. A glance at a directory had shown Green that this was a newsagent's, and it hadn't taken any brilliant deduction on his part to make him aware that it was only an address.

That in itself was enough to make him suspicious, but the name "Mary Jones" increased his feeling that there was something fishy about the transfer. Then, from what he thought was an empty jewel-case, had the certificates exhibited themselves, and somehow he half expected to read the name which he had read— "Mary Jones."

Only his natural instinct of self-preservation had enabled him to control his utter amazement, and when he once more gained the street to find the grey car and his charming client gone, he felt he could put his finger on the present possessor of the necklace.

What motive she had in posing as an inexperienced young widow he could not guess, but grimly decided that the Honourable Algy could explain if he would. It left him in the position of having been quietly relieved of twenty-five thousand pounds— a thing which was decidedly against Solomon Green's ideas of business. Consequently, it behoved him to recoup himself. To track down and get it back from the unknown woman would be a long process, with only a faint chance of success.

So far Brice and Gibbs had no idea of his suspicions, and that being so, they presented the most likely chance of reimbursing himself, providing he acted quickly. Therefore, why not strike for fifty thousand while he was at it? They would pay that as quickly as the lesser amount, and if his ideas were correct, he would never again see the necklace or the money he had loaned on it.

He had reached this decision shortly after his arrival at his offices, and was debating the wisdom of ringing up Brice and Gibbs in order to communicate to them his decision, when Brice had called him up. Green had chuckled delightedly when Brice's tones seemed to indicate that his demands would be met.

He was still immersed in thought when a clerk entered to inform him that Mr. Sexton Blake desired to see him at once. Green's mind worked like lightning. What did Blake want? In all his career he had managed not to run foul of Sexton Blake, and he could think of nothing which would bring the detective to see him, unless some angry shareholder in his latest promotion —the Golden Princess Mine —had sought Blake's assistance in order to recover his money.

In any event, he would have to see him, for if he didn't it might mean publicity —a thing which Solomon Green wanted to avoid at any price. Consequently, he told the clerk to show Blake in, and smoothed his brow in an attempt to look calm and unruffled.

Blake ignored the outstretched hand, and made no attempt to return the oily smile. He had never before come into personal contact with Solomon Green, but the promoter was listed in the Baker Street Index as a shark, and more than once he had got dangerously near to Blake's net.

He knew also that the Jew would be racking his brains as to the reason of his visit. This would make him cautious until he could feel his way, and Blake knew, if he was to succeed in cornering Green, it must be by means of a bombshell. With that idea in his mind he sat down and crossed his legs.

"Mr. Green, I wish to ask you a question," he said looking at the other with level glance.

The promoter bowed, but did not speak.

"When you handed back the jewel-case in the offices of Brice and Gibbs this morning, why didn't you pass over the same one which you received?"

Had Blake had any doubts about his choice of a question they vanished at once as he noted the result on Green. For a single moment, he stared at Blake as though frozen; then all his superficial air vanished, his jaw dropped, and the real brutal nature of the man stood out on his puffy face as he bounded up in his chair.

"What!" he yelled shrilly, in his excitement relapsing into the accent of his younger days.

"Do you wish me to repeat my question?" asked Blake coldly.

Almost as suddenly as his agitation had swept away his self-control, did Green's caution reassert itself. He closed his jaws, and, though he was breathing heavily, his features became more normal.

"I don't understand you," he managed to articulate.

"I think you do, Mr. Green."

"Do you mean to insinuate that I didn't hand back the case I received?" demanded Green blustering.

"I don't insinuate it. I state it as a fact."

"It's a lie. What have you to do with the matter, anyway?"

"I happen to be acting for Messrs. Brice and Gibbs," replied Blake quietly. "Now then, Mr. Green, you say my statement is a lie. I can prove that it isn't a lie, but the truth."

"I don't care what you can prove. I know what I am talking about. I deposited a case containing a necklace with Brice and Gibbs. I discover that it has disappeared. I want it back and in the event of its not being found, my client wants its value in cash. That is where I stand. They can put fifty detectives on the matter, but it won't alter my decision. I know nothing of it, and have stretched a point in giving them until three today to return it. If they don't do that, or pay up, I shall do as I said. To-morrow morning, as soon as I can withdraw what I have got there the whole City will know that Brice and Gibbs are not safe. Now if you want to know anything else you can go elsewhere for it."

Blake gazed dreamily at the ceiling while Green spoke, and though he felt like wringing the promoter's neck, he gave no sign. When the Jew had quite finished, and was reaching out his hand for the bell, Blake raised his arm, and spoke commandingly:

"Wait!"

"Well, what is it?"

"I wish to ask you one more question."

"I told you I would answer nothing. I'm busy."

"This is harmless enough," went on Blake coolly as he rose.

"You say you are prepared on behalf of your client to accept from the bankers the cash value of the necklace?"

"Yes."

"What is its value?"

"Fifty thousand."

"And I think you loaned twenty-five thousand on it, didn't you?"

"Yes."

"Thanks, that will be all, Mr. Green. You needn't ring, for I am leaving at once."

Nodding curtly he strode to the door, and a moment later disappeared, leaving Green a very puzzled man.

Blake's telegram to Tinker had achieved its purpose, for on emerging from Green's offices his big, grey car was waiting at the kerb, with Tinker at the wheel, and Pedro beside him. The detective entered at once and spoke in low tones.

"Drive on for a hundred yards, and pull into the kerb."

Tinker nodded, and sent the car ahead slowly until he had covered the distance. Then Blake spoke again.

"I want you to get out, my lad. Leave Pedro here. Go back to where you were waiting for me. Stay on guard there until you see Solomon Green come out. He is stout and Jewish. Dressed in morning coat, striped trousers and white waistcoat. He will also be wearing a silk hat, and carry a heavy, showy stick with a gold handle. Both hands are loaded with diamonds. You can't mistake him.

"Follow him wherever he goes. If he enters any places note the addresses, and if he stops to speak with anyone, try if possible to hear what he says. The matter is urgent, so report to me as quickly as possible. If you find out anything which seems important send me urgent wires whenever the opportunity presents itself."

"All right, guv'nor. I'll spot him and keep on his heels. I'll send all wires to Baker Street?"

"Yes, I shall wait there for them. Understand, it is urgent, so don't let him give you the slip."

As soon as Tinker had sped away, Blake took the wheel and started the car for Baker Street, for he desired the atmosphere of the consulting-room in which to turn over in his mind one or two points which his interview with Solomon Green had raised.

Once there he lost no time in filling his pipe, and with Pedro stretched out at his feet, began marshalling the facts one by one.

"One thing is certain," he muttered, puffing a heavy cloud of smoke upwards. "Until I told him, Solomon Green had no idea that there were two black cases in the matter. If I am not mistaken that will upset him considerably, for I'll wager anything he doesn't himself know the whereabouts of his client.

"For some reason, someone has swindled Green out of twenty-five thousand pounds, and rather than lose it he is trying to hold up Brice and Gibbs for it. The point is who is this mysterious client, and where can she be found? Again, what has become of the original jewel-case, and when was the change made? It seems safe to assume that it was the original case which Green took from the offices of Brice and Gibbs. The most likely theory seems that he made the exchange himself on the way, but I don't think so. The genuineness of his agitation is against that, as well as his surprise at seeing the share certificates in the case when he opened it at the bank.

"Taking the hypothesis that the exchange was not made by him, and granting the truth of his statement that the seal was only broken in his office, and in the presence of his client and clerk, what is the explanation of the fact that the necklace was even then missing? I must confess that it is one of the most puzzling affairs I have ever come across. The very facts seem to contradict themselves.

"By keeping a close watch upon Green, I shall be able to discover whether he is lying or not, but if he stole the gems before reaching his office, then why didn't he know about the second case? That is the knotty point. Brice knows nothing of its existence either, and that brings the proposition around to the mysterious client again.

"If she stole her own necklace, and made the transfer of the jewel-cases then when and how did she manage it? If the gems had been in the original case when Green opened it, then the theory could be advanced that she had managed to exchange the cases when his back was turned, but that is impossible, because the case was empty.

"However, I am very much inclined to think that she was clever enough to do the trick in some way, and that only can be proved by running her to earth. If she has engineered this affair, and has succeeded in swindling Green out of that lump of money then she has more brains than the average individual. It almost smacks of Mademoiselle Yvonne, but it seems unlikely that she should be mixed up with Green in any way.

"If that is the case then Green, being in ignorance of her whereabouts, intends recouping himself by common blackmail. At any rate if nothing develops to-night, I think I can prevent him from carrying out his threat to-morrow morning. He can't stand too much publicity, and I think the mention of one or two facts will cause him to reconsider.

"I shall be on hand in any event, and if he proves too stubborn then Brice and Gibbs must pay over the fifty thousand, and leave the recovery of it in my hands. I don't think it would take long to corner Mr. Green if I set out to do it. However, something may develop to-night, and then—"

His musings were interrupted as a loud rat-tat came at the door, and rising, he went along to answer it. It was a boy with a telegram, and on regaining the consulting-room he tore it open. The code told him at once that it was from Tinker.

Tinker took to his heels and bolted away for dear life, with the sound of a revolver shot ringing in his ears.

AS soon as Blake had departed, Solomon Green leaned back, and wiped his forehead with a gigantic handkerchief.

"Now what the dickens is his game?" he muttered. "Brice and Gibbs must have 'phoned for him as soon as I left. What does he mean by asking me why I didn't hand back the same case as I received? That must be pure bluff in order to frighten me off, but I'll show them how much that child's game will work with me.

"There was only one case, and how that cursed woman managed to get hold of the necklace under my very eyes beats me. Brice is innocent enough, but that is no reason why they shouldn't stand the loss."

At that moment his eyes fell on the packet of certificates, which he had found on opening the case at the bankers. For a moment he stared at them, then he leaned forward tensely.

"By thunder!" he muttered. "I wonder if that fellow Sexton Blake was not bluffing after all? If there weren't two cases used, how in blazes did those certificates get where they were? Who put them there, and where did they come from? It's a funny thing that I felt something queer last week when I got that letter from Bayes telling me he had sold out his interest in the Golden Princess; and now these certificates appear as mysteriously as the necklace has vanished. Moreover, they cost him exactly the same amount as I loaned on that necklace.

"By heavens! Is there after all any connection between the two, and is he a party to the swindle? How they managed it I can't make out. Anyway, with Blake on the matter it's going to be risky pushing Brice for the fifty thousand. If I can lay my finger on a weak spot in this I'll make Bayes sweat for it."

With a smothered imprecation Green rose and stuffed the bundle of certificates back in his pocket. Then he got his hat, and moved to the door, muttering:

"I'll try it! I'll try it!"

With that he hastened out, and, on reaching the street, hired a taxi. Even if he hadn't been so absorbed in his thoughts it is doubtful if he would have noticed the slim lad who slipped into another taxi and sped along after him.

Green's first objective was to follow up a suggestion which had been presenting itself all day. That was to endeavour to locate the mysterious young widow who had played ducks and drakes so successfully with him, Solomon Green, the man who was reputed to be the very incarnation of sharp practice.

He had only put off doing so because Brice and Gibbs offered a much easier, as well as a much more profitable source of reimbursement. Blake's entry into the affair had been disturbing, however, and his own recent endorsement of the detective's statement, that there were two black jewel-cases had filled him with a vague, though none the less alarming, feeling that his chances of holding up Brice and Gibbs were far less rosy than he had thought.

As far as any concrete plan was concerned it did not exist with him. He was completely at sea, and felt that, unless he played his cards very carefully, Solomon Green would be a loser of twenty-five thousand pounds.

The share certificates had disturbed him also, for he knew quite well that if they had only been returned as a technical substitute for the money, he dare not invoke the law to punish the swindlers. Since he himself had promoted the mine, and had sold the shares as being worth the money paid for them, he could not very well get up in court and say now that they were worthless, even though the mine was going into the receiver's hands.

It would draw too much attention to his latest promotion, and the details would be in every paper. His cross-examination would bring out many details which he had no desire to make public; and, although he had successfully defended several suits already, another appearance in court would hardly be looked upon favourably. In view of his record and past trials, he would stand little chance, and he knew it.

For these several reasons he knew, if he recouped himself, it must be by strategy and nothing else.

His taxi drove into the courtyard of the Hotel Knickerbocker and drew up. Tinker, in the taxi behind, did likewise, and when Green passed under the imposing portals between two gorgeously-clad commissionaires the lad was close behind.

The promotor made his way at once to the inquiry desk. Tinker grabbed a timetable from a rack near at hand and followed.

While Green interrogated the clerk the lad stood idly by reading his timetable, and so natural had his movements been that Green never for a moment suspected he was other than a guest of the hotel who didn't matter.

"Is Mrs. Carter still here?" asked Green.

"One moment, sir," replied the man.

Turning, he threw open a large guest-book, and with nimble fingers turned the pages to the letter "C." Then he ran his index finger down a list of names on several pages, finally stopping at a name near the bottom of the page.

"No, sir," he said, turning back to Green. "She arrived here a week ago and left this morning."

"Do you know where she went?"

"No, sir; there is no indication here."

"Did she leave any instructions with regard to the forwarding of letters?"

"I'll see, sir."

Once more the clerk turned, this time opening a smaller book. After a few minutes' examination of its pages he looked up.

"There is no entry of any description regarding letters, sir."

"Then if I addressed a letter here you would have to hold it until you received instructions?"

"Yes, sir."

Green turned, and from his vantage point Tinker could see that he wore a look of mingled anger and disappointment. He strode frowningly to the door, and, dropping his timetable on a stand near by, the lad went after him.

Green's taxi was already drawing away when Tinker reached the courtyard, and, jumping into his own, he signed to the driver to follow the other.

From there the chase led along the Strand until they reached Trafalgar Square. From that point Green's taxi went swiftly along until it made Piccadilly Circus, and, threading its way through the traffic there, kept on up Piccadilly.

Tinker's driver almost lost it in the Circus, but picked it up again, and turned inquiringly to his fare as Green's driver drew into the kerb in front of the Junior Exchange Club.

Tinker made a quick sign for the man to keep on, and then, rapping on the window, pointed to the opposite kerb.

From the position in which they were he could see the entrance to the club, and barely had he turned his eyes in that direction, when he saw his quarry run up the steps, and the taxi he had used turn away and go back down Piccadilly.

Then it was that Tinker drew out a sheet of paper, and began writing swiftly in code. It was the telegram which Blake received while immersed in his deductions at Baker Street, and, translated, read as follows:

"Quarry left his office soon after you. Took taxi, and went to Hotel Knickerbocker. Was able to follow him closely. He went at once to inquiry desk. Asked for a Mrs. Carter. Clerk informed him she had arrived a week ago and left that morning. Quarry looked angry and disappointed. Went out at once, and took taxi to Junior Exchange Club. Dismissed taxi. Is in there now. Will keep on trail."

As soon as he had finished writing the message Tinker stepped from the cab and handed it to the chauffeur.

"Will you send that as an urgent wire for me?" he asked.

"Yes, sir."

"Thanks. Here's a sovereign. Keep any change there may be."

"Will you want me again, sir?"

"Well, after you send the wire you had better return. If I'm not here don't wait. On the other hand, you managed to keep that other taxi in sight pretty successfully, and I might want you to follow another."

"All right, sir. I'll send this from Haymarket and return immediately."

Tinker nodded, and as the man drove off the lad slipped back against the railings, and in the shelter of a tree continued his surveillance of the club.

It was now late afternoon, and in the crowds which were passing and repassing he knew there was little danger of Green noticing him.

"I'd give something to know what he went in there for," he muttered. "I wonder what the case is, anyway. It must have something to do with that appointment the guv'nor's had with Brice and Gibbs, the bankers. I wonder if the old fellow has been passing crook paper, or what? Anyway, he won't give me the slip if I know it."

Had the lad been able to follow Green inside the club he would have gained a little more light on the matter.

How Solomon Green had ever become a member of the Junior Exchange Club was a mystery to many. The truth of the matter was that during a meeting, when only a bare quorum of the committee were present, he had been put through.

Those who had voted for him were all more or less indebted to him for money and favours. Green had seen to that, and as no one had taken the trouble since then to object, a member he had remained.

On the present occasion he passed along the big entrance hall, and made direct for the smoking-room. As always at that hour of the day, and particularly at that time of year, it was far from crowded. One or two here and there nodded shortly to Green who, contrary to his usual custom, bowed frigidly in return.

As he walked down the room his eyes swept over the occupants of the comfortable chairs, until they rested on a young man sitting by himself.

His legs were crossed indolently. He held a glass of whisky and soda in one hand, and a cigarette in the other. He was gazing out at the passing crowds in lazy fashion, from time to time taking a languid puff at his cigarette, or a short sip from the glass. He made a picture of perfect content.

The sight evidently did not tend to put Solomon Green in any better humour, for it was the Honourable Algernon Montague Bayes. Coming to a pause directly behind the chair, Green bent over, and said softly:

"Good-afternoon, Mr. Bayes!"

The Honourable Algy was a poor actor, and a much less discerning man could have read the truth in his actions when he heard that voice over his shoulder.

As though a bomb had suddenly exploded beneath his chair he shot upwards, sending the glass crashing to the floor. Turning round, he gazed at Green with startled eyes; then, gathering his wits together, he smiled crookedly, and stammered;

"Oh—er—good-afternoon, Mr. Green!"

"I seem to have startled you."

"Er —yes, a trifle. Getting decidedly nervous lately. Must have a blow in the country for a bit. How's business? Will you sit down?"

Green smiled with as pleasant an expression as he could command. He had read in the other's startled manner as much of the truth of matters as he hoped now to find out from him. Bayes had himself in hand, and nothing was to be gained by alarming him too much. A precipitate move might spoil everything, and now that he felt confident there was a very big connection between Bayes and the missing necklace, he thought he was quite clever enough to turn it to his own benefit.

"Thanks," he said, still smiling. "I just dropped in for a drink. Sorry I gave you such a start."

"Oh, that's all right! Unfortunate about the Golden Princess."

"Yes. I felt quite upset when I wrote you, but I got a cable from the manager to-day that the situation had changed entirely."

"Struck it rich?"

"Rather!" replied Green, lying glibly. "He has struck a saddle formation, which he says is simply reeking with the stuff."

"Good! The shareholders will be pleased!"

"Yes, it will be a pleasant surprise to them. It's too bad you sold your shares now."

"I should say so. I felt sorry I had done so when I realised the mine had petered out. In fact, I felt like taking them back and returning the money."

"By the way, was it to a friend? I received your letter, giving the name and address, but it has slipped my memory."

"Until I sold them I had never met the purchaser before in my life," answered Bayes.

"Ah, quite so!" murmured Green. "Well, I must be getting along. I'll send you particulars of any new thing that comes to my notice, Mr. Bayes. Perhaps you would like to reinvest in the Golden Princess?"

"Not just at present. However, I shall be glad to hear of anything good."

"Thanks. I'll let you know."

"Now, I wonder what his game is?" mused the Honourable Algy, as Green rose and strolled out. "He never mentioned receiving those certificates, and Mademoiselle Yvonne palmed them off on him this morning. He's a deep one. He never comes here in the afternoon, and I'm not such a fool that I can't perceive he came to see me.

"I wonder why he put up that tale about the mine turning out rich? Did he think I'd be fool enough to reinvest in it, and did he hope to get back his twenty-five thousand in that way? It means a development of some kind, anyway, and it's too much for me. I'll hop round this evening to Queen Anne's Gate, and tell Graves and Mademoiselle Yvonne just what has occurred. They may be able to see the meaning of it."

And therein the Hon. Algy made exactly the decision which Green was hoping he would make.

On reaching the street Solomon Green stood on the kerb, and gazed about him for a few minutes. Then he started picking his way across Piccadilly, and Tinker, who still stood on guard, felt a queer little thrill run through him as he saw Green coming directly towards him.

The lad grew more puzzled than ever when the Jew took up his stand near the same spot, and purchasing a paper, began calmly reading it. Tinker's taxi had returned, and was waiting. When he had seen Green emerging from the club, he had prepared to follow him at once, but now all his plans were upset. There was his quarry standing not three feet away from him, calmly smoking and reading the paper.

Tinker didn't know whether he had discovered that the lad was following him and was coolly standing him out, or whether he was waiting for someone himself.

Then, suddenly, while the lad surreptitiously watched, he saw Green gaze over the top of the paper in the direction of the club entrance. Again and again he did this, and Tinker realised that he was watching for someone to come out.

"This is certainly getting complicated," muttered the lad to himself, as he also purchased a paper. "I'd give something to know what the guv'nor has dropped on to. I wonder if he expected this development. Anyway, I'll pop him off another wire about it as soon as I get a chance. He said it was urgent, and by the look of things I guess it is."

For over an hour Tinker and his unconscious quarry stood there. It was now crawling on for seven o'clock, and the lights were twinkling, hanging in long pale lines, and casting a blurred reflection on the newly-watered roadway. Dusk had already conquered the narrow lanes, and soon would creep over the broader streets, and turn the grey bulk of the buildings to black. Then the parks—the last city stronghold of day—would succumb, and night would spread her mantle of mystery over the great teeming, pulsing stretch of the city.

Already Piccadilly was cleared of its afternoon crowds. The clubs, and further up towards Hyde Park Corner, the stately houses were alight. Great windows gave a glimpse of club comforts, lounging men and noiselessly moving waiters. The theatre crush had not started yet. The Ritz, Prince's, and the Piccadilly were brilliantly lighted, casting forth an atmosphere of luxury borne on the fugitive strains of an orchestra.

Omnibuses loaded with home-going toilers, too accustomed to or too tired to heed their surroundings, clattered by in an endless stream. Far down past Prince's could be seen the glare of Piccadilly Circus, looking like a monster merry-go-round, in which horses, taxis, omnibuses and human beings played the part of bobbing figures.

Overhead, the stars were lost in the heavy blanket of the city smoke, and only a few blazing sky-signs told the spot where a tall building ended its skyward career.

Piccadilly! the thoroughfare of light and pleasure and laughter, the thoroughfare of sorrows, misery and tears, embracing generations of each —cold, warm, dark, light —everything to all men, the richly-flowing artery of the greatest city in the world.

Something of this sort passed through Tinker's mind as the coming night forced him to fold up his paper. As he stood there in the great stream, a chip, which for the moment had clung to its bank, the lad felt to the full how utterly alone one could be in the midst of millions.

His thoughts went back to the days when he had tasted of that bitter cup, and a great wave of thankfulness welled up in him as he thought of the man who had changed his life from that misery to a life of hope and happiness and to a career. He thought of the cosy rooms at Baker Street, and of the great faithful dog; and even with the thought came a sudden realisation of the great pity it was that men schemed and plotted against their fellow-creatures like the savages of prehistoric days, living and dying without breaking through the crust of greed and selfishness and envy into the more beautiful atmosphere of honesty, cheerfulness and unselfishness.

He wondered vaguely if men like Solomon Green ever thought of anything but the acquisition of money, and then a move on that gentleman's part jerked him out of his reverie. Once more he was the keen lad, every instinct on the alert.

Green had tossed away his paper, and was holding up his hand for a taxi. Tinker was still lounging against the railings, but his gaze swept the steps of the club in search of what had caused Green to move.

He could see a figure descending, but it was getting too dark to make out the features. At that moment Green entered a taxi, which had pulled in to the kerb, and Tinker, satisfied that if he succeeded in keeping his original quarry in sight, he would also learn something of the other man, spoke hurriedly to his own driver, and jumped in.

The theatre crush had now begun, and it was by no means as easy to follow a taxi through the streets as it had been in daylight. The Honourable Algy —for it was his appearance which had started Green into activity —was evidently in no hurry, not suspicious of being followed. His driver took things leisurely, and after a short time, turned off into a quieter thoroughfare.

In this fashion the little procession drove on to Queen Anne's Gate. There the Honourable Algy alighted, and dismissed his cab. Running up the steps which led to Yvonne's residence he disappeared within the entrance, and Tinker's driver drove in just as Green's taxi drew in to the spot vacated by the first cab.

Green also disappeared in the wake of Bayes, and Tinker signalled to his driver to pull up. Looking back, he could see that Green had also dismissed his taxi, so not knowing what the next move might be, Tinker decided to do the same.

Before putting his decision into practice, however, he stepped forward under the light, and hurriedly wrote another urgent wire to Blake. Like the previous one, it was in code, and read:

"Quarry came out of Club over an hour ago. Walked across and stood right near me. Decided he was waiting for someone, and was right. His quarry came out few minutes ago. Both have entered 42B, Queen Anne's Gate. Don't know which apartment, but will endeavour to follow. If I succeed, will drop four matches on floor outside door I have entered, in case you should come on."

Handing this to the driver, who promised to send it at once, he paid him, and making his way along in the shadow, he hurried up the steps and entered the door through which the other two were gone.

As he did so, he was just in time to hear voices on the right, and to see Green disappearing through a door on the right, then it closed, and he was left standing alone in the big entrance hall.

He realised that he must make a move quickly if he were to discover what was going on inside where Green had entered; and he presumed the first man was there as well. He could see nobody about, but another door on the left told him there was another residence there, and a lift well argued the same thing for the floors above.

Somebody might come at any moment, for it was still early in the evening, but he had his revolver with him. This he shifted into his coat pocket, then, with a final look around, stole softly across to the door on the right.

A glance showed it to be a lock which sprang when the door was closed, but under Blake's tuition he had learned not to be baulked for long by things of that description. His greatest fear was that somebody might come before he succeeded in getting in. Although he could easily explain such a compromising position to the police, still the complication would cause him to lose sight of his quarry, and that he knew was exactly what Blake did not want him to do.

First he drew out a box of matches, and taking out four dropped them near the door, close against the wall, where they would escape general notice, but would be visible to Blake in case he came. Then, thrusting the box back into his pocket, he drew out a tiny, spidery-looking steel instrument, and with infinite caution inserted one of its delicate claws in the keyhole.

He succeeded in passing it in noiselessly, and in fact, his pulses were hammering so with the tension that he felt they must drown any sound made by the instrument. He breathed a sigh of relief as the lock turned back, and easing back the instrument, he softly withdrew it and thrust it into his pocket.

Then, gripping his revolver, he pushed open the door and passed through, not knowing what the interior might hold for him. Blackness met him, and drawing a deep breath, he stepped through, every nerve tense, his hearing strained and his heart beating quickly. He gently closed the door and felt for the opposite wall.

Then he stood for a few moments, peering through the darkness. Suddenly he caught the sound of voices, and, as his eyes grew more accustomed to the darkness, he could see a thin crack of light far down the hall in which he stood.

Dropping to his knees, he put one hand against the wall, and, with his revolver in the other, began creeping along. Twice he had to move round, once when his hand encountered a small table, and again when he felt a chair. Beyond that the way was clear, when, as the crack of light was barely three feet ahead, the wall suddenly ended, and his hand sank inwards against heavy portieres.

"Another room," he muttered, as he groped about. "No door. Only these curtains. No light. It couldn't be better for my purpose."

He got cautiously to his feet and pushed aside the portieres. Then he stood behind them just inside the door, and found that by drawing them apart at the side nearest the crack of light he was within a foot of a closed door and could hear what was being said. Holding his breath he thrust his head out into the hall and bent to listen.

As he did so, a light mocking laugh met him, and as he heard the words which followed, he stiffened and breathed excitedly, for he had heard that voice too often not to know to whom it belonged.

"Mademoiselle Yvonne," he whispered, bending still closer. Gee! the guv'nor is certainly a wonder. How did he drop on to this?"

Then he gave his full attention to the voice.

"You are more clever than I thought, Mr. Green." he heard Yvonne say mockingly. "Who would have thought you would track down the poor little widow so soon?"

"By heavens! you will find you have tackled the wrong man," he heard a voice reply savagely, and rightly judged it to be Green's.

"Do you think so?" laughed Yvonne. "Really, Mr. Green, you are too droll. What do you expect to gain by coming here?"

"I want that necklace back."

"What makes you think I have it? Didn't you bring the sealed case from the bankers and open it yourself, only to find it empty? The fact of the matter is, Mr. Green, any court of law would support my claim against you for its full value."

"I don't care about that. How you got it I don't know, but I want it back. If you think I am going to stand for this kind of thing, you are mistaken. And you, Bayes, may think yourself clever in taking a part in this, but you will find yourself in trouble."

"Never mind Mr. Bayes," replied Yvonne. "This matter is between you and me, Mr. Green. What made you think of following Mr. Bayes?"

"Because, when I got back to the bank and opened the case, I found it full of share certificates bearing his name. Now then, come, Mrs. Carter, or whatever your real name is. Either hand over the necklace and redeem it properly, or give me my twenty-five thousand. I won't ask again."

"Really, I seem to be a most wonderful person, Mr. Green. First you accuse me of spiriting away a necklace from a sealed case, and now you accuse me of placing a bundle of share certificates in that case in the same mysterious manner."

"No, I don't. You used two cases of similar appearance."

"Ah! what makes you think that?" and as Yvonne asked the question, Tinker could hear the sudden change in her tones.

"Never mind how I know it. Do you propose to pay up?"

"Certainly not, Mr. Green. And since you forced your way in here without permission, I think you had better leave, I refuse to discuss the matter any further. I make a contra demand upon you for the necklace or its value. That is final. Now go!"

A short silence followed, the reason for which Tinker could not guess. He imagined Green was debating his next move, but that was hardly the case.

In the room in which the conversation was taking place were Yvonne, Graves, Bayes, and Green. The first three had just begun to discuss the Honourable Algy's news of Green's call at the club, when a ring had come at the door, and before the servant could prevent him, Green had forced his way in.

The conversation which had taken place before Tinker gained his vantage point behind the portieres was of much the same tenor as that which he had heard. Until that moment, however, Green had been too much excited to take special notice of his surroundings. As he gazed about him after Yvonne's last remark, however, his eyes fell on a soft black leather case which lay on a table within a few feet of him. It was his utter stupefaction which had caused the silence which Tinker had put down to a different cause.

The silence now broke suddenly into pandemonium. In the room, Green, driven to the last point by Yvonne's mocking words, had actually been on the point of retiring, when his eyes fell on the case. It was exactly similar to the one containing the necklace, and he hadn't the shadow of a doubt but that it was that very one and no other.

The sight of it so close to him snapped the last thread of his self-control, and before any of the others could prevent him he gave a loud cry of rage, and leaped forward. Grasping the case, he rushed to the door, and before either of the occupants of the room could prevent him, or Tinker could withdraw his head, Green had the door open.

In a single flash Tinker got a view of a richly-furnished room, of Yvonne standing against a table in a shimmering gown of blue, looking like a rare painting, of Graves lounging in an easy chair, and of a younger man sitting opposite to him. Then his vision registered the flying figure of the man whom he had followed, as the three figures behind Green woke into action, and Bayes cried excitedly:

"The case!"

Tinker saw a small black article in the hand of the oncoming man. His eyes took all this in during the moment occupied by Green in throwing open the door. He was nearly upon Tinker, and would almost brush him as he flew by. Quick as lightning the lad jerked his head back and shot out a hand.

Fortune was with him, for as Green's hand containing the case dashed by, Tinker's fingers grasped it; he gave a jerk, and before the astonished Green could possibly have imagined what had become of it Tinker had dropped the curtain and was standing, with thundering pulses, in the shelter of the dark room.

Whatever Green thought he did not stop to investigate, but kept on at top speed. A mighty crash told that he had come a cropper over something in the dark hall; then the others swept by, a shot rang out, another great crash followed as Graves took a header over the same article of furniture which had upset Green.

Then came a confusion of noises, followed by Yvonne's clear tones, the front door banged fiercely, there was a great clatter of footsteps on the tiled floor in the big entrance hall of the building as the chase emerged from the flat, then more shouts, followed again by fainter sounds, the echo of flying feet along the street, then silence!

Tinker had stood as motionless as a statue during those few moments. Only the darkness of the hall, into which his head projected, had saved him from being seen when Green threw open the door of the lighted room. What had impelled him to reach out and grasp the case as the fugitive sped by, he did not know. He had acted on the spur of the moment, and the result was that Green would be utterly unable to imagine what mysterious hand had shot out through the darkness and jerked it from his grasp.

Neither Yvonne, Graves, nor Bayes had seen the action, and all thought Green still had it. Determined not to let him escape with it, they had risked a street chase, leaving Tinker alone in the house possessing the black case which, from what he had heard, seemed to be the bone of contention.

"I wonder if this has any bearing on what the guv'nor is investigating?" he muttered, as he parted the curtains and peered out. "I shouldn't be at all surprised if it has. Anyway, that was a lucky grab, and as it's useless for me to follow Green now, I'd better be getting out of this while I have the chance."

He slipped through into the hall, and began making his way along. Up at the other end he could see a narrow, perpendicular line of light, showing that in their haste to overtake Green they had not fully closed the door. The gloom was thus broken sufficiently for him to see where he was going, and a tumbled heap at one side in the shape of an overturned chair was visible proof of the place at which Green had come a cropper.

Tinker's mind was rapidly turning over the surprising situation, into which he had landed. What was meant by the "case" and the "necklace" in the conversation he had overheard he had only a vague idea. To him it was evident that Yvonne and Green were at loggerheads over the matter, and the mention of the bankers made him feel fairly certain that it must be the same affair on which Blake was working. Had there been any doubt in his mind, the surprising entry of Yvonne into the evening would have lent colour to that theory.

Who Bayes was, he did not know, nor could he guess his connection with the matter. He imagined he must be the man whom Green had followed from the Junior Exchange Club, and therein he was right. For a moment he was sorely tempted to enter the lighted room and await Yvonne's return; but remembering Blake's explicit instructions, he decided it was best to retain the case, make his escape before the others returned, and leave the settlement of matters to his master.

He chuckled softly as he thought of Yvonne, Graves, and Bayes tearing after the empty-handed Green; then he went ahead cautiously, and laid his hand on the door. Just as he did so he caught the murmur of voices, followed by the sound of footsteps coming along the tiled entrance hall of the building.

For a tense moment he stood rigid as a statue, the leather case in one hand, and his other on the handle of the door. On came the footsteps, and louder grew the voices. He recognised Yvonne's above the others, and turning swiftly, he sped silently down the hall in the direction of the dark room where he had been concealed.

As luck would have it, he forgot about the overturned chair. With a grunt, he struck it full, and went tumbling headlong over it. The crash resounded loudly through the house, and an excited exclamation at the door told him Yvonne and her companions had been alarmed by it.

Scrambling to his feet, he started on again. The case had become unfastened when he fell and snapping-to the lid again as he ran, he reached the portieres which hung over the door of the dark room, jerked them aside, and tore across to a faint square, which indicated the location of the window —just as a scurry of footsteps sounded behind him.

Tinker knew he was done for if the window was fastened by any sort of patent catch, but, nevertheless, he didn't intend to give in without a struggle. Feverishly he worked, and uttered a gasp of relief as his fingers succeeded in forcing back the catch. Then he stuffed the case in his pocket, and threw up the window.

At that moment the curtains over the door flew apart, and suddenly the whole room was flooded with light. Tinker sat with one leg over the window-sill, wondering how far was the drop to the ground.

He could see Yvonne standing with one hand on the switch, and holding in the other a small automatic. Behind her crowded Graves and Bayes, every one of them having intense surprise written on their faces.

Tinker took one look, grinned cheerfully, and leaped just as Yvonne and the others tore after him.

It was more of a drop than he had imagined, and the pavement below being asphalte he was shaken badly, but uninjured. Getting to his feet, he tore across towards a fence some twenty yards before him, realising, as he panted on, that he was in the rear courtyard of the block of mansions.

The shot fired by Yvonne when Green had grabbed the case and attempted to get away with it had evidently aroused other residents of the building, for as he went past some basement windows another shot sounded, some windows flew up, and the cry "Stop thief!" rang out from half a dozen points at once.

The lad's fighting blood was up now, and he grimly determined that unless some unforeseen hindrance came he would make the alley in the rear safely, and once there he knew a dozen ways of shaking off pursuit. Just then the rear wall loomed up, and keeping beside it, he raced along looking for the gate.

A moment later he had it, and lifting the latch pushed hard. It was, however, locked firmly, and as footsteps sounded on the asphalte behind him, followed by increased cries, he dropped the latch and turned to the right. Suddenly he ran full tilt into something, and staggered back, half stunned by the shock.

Someone behind sent a light wavering about the yard at the same moment, and while he stood recovering his senses it fell full on Tinker. The cries multiplied, the stampede after him was resumed, and escape seemed impossible.

The same light which had revealed the fugitive, however, had shown him the way of escape, for he could see that he had fetched up against a coal cellar. Before him was a low window. In desperation, he lifted his fist, and sent it crashing through a pane of glass.

Disregarding the warm trickling of blood on his knuckles, he grasped the sash, and pulled himself up until his feet rested on the sill. Then gripping the edge of the roof, he lifted his foot, used the broken sash as a stirrup, and giving a heave, landed sprawling, on the top of the shed.

As he had imagined, the building was built against the rear wall, the roof being flush with the top of it. The crash of glass behind him told him a pursuer was essaying to climb as he had done, and the dancing light further back showed where others were endeavouring to open the gate and head him off.

Nearly exhausted, he half rolled, half tumbled over the wall to the ground outside. Then scrambling to his feet, he tore along at full speed just as a police whistle sounded somewhere behind. In five minutes he had taken a dozen turnings, the sounds of pursuit had died away, and he pulled up, panting, as he reached a quiet, residential street.

"Scott! That was hot!" he gasped, leaning against a pillar-box and examining his injured hand. "I didn't mind the police, but I'd never have got away with the case if they had landed me. I don't think Mademoiselle Yvonne recognised me, but I can't tell. If not, they will probably think I was a confederate of Green's. Anyway, I'll make tracks for Baker Street, and see what the guv'nor thinks of the whole fracas."

Straightening up, he felt to assure himself that the case was safe, then wrapping his handkerchief about his cut knuckles, he walked along until he turned into a larger thoroughfare. There he hailed a taxi, and entering, told the driver to go to Baker Street.

A quarter of an hour later he made his way up the steps and along to the consulting-room, expecting to see Blake. There was, however, no sign of his master, and a hurried examination of the rooms showed Pedro to be the only occupant.

Returning to the consulting-room, Tinker drew the black case from his pocket, and laid it on the desk. Then he turned and sought the bath-room, where he bathed his hand and rebandaged it. With an anticipatory smile on his face, he went back and picked up the case.

"Now," he muttered cheerfully, "we'll see what has caused all the excitement. Ah, here's the catch! Come cn —open up, and let us have a look at what you contain!"

The catch sprang back, the lid flew up, and Tinker bent forward to see —nothing!

Sexton Blake discovers the overturned chair in Yvonne's flat.

The Seventh Chapter. Blake Has a Quiet Smoke in Yvonne's Flat ——And Discovers the Secret of the Case.

WHILE Tinker had been involved in such a surprising situation as an outcome of his trailing Solomon Green, Blake showed little signs of being engaged on a case which by the very necessity of things must be brought to some concrete form by the following morning.

Ever since receiving Tinker's first telegram, which the taxi driver had sent from Haymarket, Blake had apparently given no thought to the case whatever. He had calmly read until dinner, had dined early, then had lighted his pipe and resumed his book.

Those who knew Sexton Blake would have known that, though the case had been put from his mind for the present, it was only because his mental analysis of the meagre facts had taken him as far as it was possible to go.

This analysis, it will be remembered, had brought him to the point where he felt convinced Solomon Green was as ignorant of the existence of two black cases as was Brice. Also, it had pointed the arrow of suspicion at Green's mysterious client, and, though he had said little in his interview with the promoter, Blake had gauged his remarks exactly in order that they might have the required effect— namely, to cause Solomon Green to make a move. Therein Blake felt was the only logical continuance of the matter.

If Green were, as Blake thought, ignorant of the whereabouts of the supposed Mrs. Carter, then the detective's statement regarding the two cases, and his almost imperceptibly accusatory tone to Green, would make the latter disturbed over Blake's entry into the affair, and also make him less certain of weeding Brice and Gibbs for the money.

That would cause him to search for his mysterious client, with the hope of having two strings to his bow, and what Blake planned for with the forethought and care of a general who knows not the position of the enemy, was exactly what came to pass. Tinker's first wire proved that, and, unless something very unforeseen occurred, Blake knew a second and perhaps even a third wire must come.

It was still early in the evening when the lad's second telegram arrived. This told Blake what had occurred up to the time when Tinker had seen Solomon Green disappear within the entrance of the building at Queen Anne's Gate.

Then all his indolence dropped from him in a flash. Once more he was the deductive machine, the analytical mentality, the mathematical detective. Instantly all the facts were again foremost in his mind, and, having spun his web, he now moved to catch the prey which would become entangled in it.

He moved briskly. First, his revolver went into his pocket, then a slouch hat was put on his head, which, when drawn down, effectually concealed the upper part of his face. Next, he drew from his desk a small steel instrument, similar to that which Tinker had used, and, stuffing an electric torch in the pocket of his coat, he spoke sharply to Pedro, telling him to look after things, and started out.

Reaching the street he hailed a taxi and gave the address—Queen Anne's Gate. He had no idea what he was to find there. Green may have gone there as friend or foe. The man Tinker mentioned in his wire, and whom Green had tracked, might be the key of the situation.

It certainly seemed that he must have some important bearing on the matter, for the Jew had started out so soon after the detective's departure. Then the call at the club and the wait outside were suspicious to Blake. But he felt positive the next step in the game lay within the walls of that building at Queen Anne's Gate.

About the time Blake caught the taxi and left Baker Street Tinker was racing through the courtyard at the rear of the house at Queen Anne's Gate with a dozen pursuers on his heels. He had not been mistaken when he thought he heard a policeman's whistle behind him for Yvonne's shots had brought a burly representative of the law hurrying up.

To him, as to the other tenants of the building, Yvonne explained that her place had been entered by burglars, that one had escaped by way of the front door, and that they had chased him only to see him get away.

On their return they had discovered that a confederate had managed to conceal himself, and they found him about to leave. Then the chase had taken place, and, having no police-whistle, she had fired her revolver in the air.

This explanation took place in the rear lane of the mansions, and not one of her hearers dreamed of questioning the story of the beautiful girl who resided in the building with her uncle. The constable accompanied them back to the apartments, and waited until

Yvonne made a pretence of searching to see if anything was missing.

It was no part of her plan to have the law interest itself in her affairs, and, though she knew one of the escaped intruders had got away with the necklace, she gave the officer to understand that everything was all right.

After a few more preliminaries he departed, and no sooner had the door closed than Yvonne acted with all her old decision. The servants, who were also members of her "circle," slept on the top floor of the mansions where rooms were set apart for all the servants of the tenants. Private bells ran from the apartment to each servant's room, and one of these Yvonne rang. Then she turned to Graves.

"We have no time to lose," she said tensely. "That necklace must be recovered to-night. Either Green or the other has managed to get away with it, and we must head them off. The only plan I can think of right now is to locate Green. I have rung for Alec. You, uncle, take him and motor out at once to Green's house. Wait there until he arrives. I don't think he will get there before you. If he doesn't turn up the only thing to do is to return here. Will you come with me, Mr. Bayes, or would you rather not get mixed up in this?"

"I'll come, rather," he replied earnestly. "You've got into this thing over helping me, mademoiselle, and I'm going to see it through."

"Thanks," she said, putting out her hand and smiling one of her adorable smiles.

At that moment Alec appeared, and listened stolidly to his mistress's instructions. Then he and Graves departed, and a moment later, when Yvonne had wrapped herself in a long dark cloak, she and the Honourable Algy followed.

They had barely vanished on their different missions when Blake's taxi drew up at the kerb and the detective descended. Dismissing the man, he mounted the steps and stood for a moment in the entrance hall. Then he turned and walked across to the door on the left.

A few moments served to convince him that the guiding matches had not been dropped there. Turning, he approached the door on the right, and a gleam of satisfaction came into his eyes as he saw four matches in close against the wall.

"Good boy!" he breathed. "Now, what is behind that door? Has Tinker gained an entrance or has his man left? What a tantalising thing that door is. Well, here goes!"

He raised his hand and put his finger on the bell, then he pressed. For a full minute he stood waiting and listening, but could hear no sound of movement inside. Again he pressed, this time longer —again no answer. After waiting two minutes he gave the bell two short, sharp rings, then a long one. Dead silence met him, and, with a shrug, he returned to the street. He walked along a few steps and gazed up at the windows.

"Every room in darkness," he muttered. "What has happened? If Tinker had left it seems to me he would have removed one match and left three, knowing I would read the meaning. But the original four are. still there, which says he has not emerged from that door since he entered. I'll ring again, and if there is no answer this time I'll do a little housebreaking."

Suiting the action to the word Blake retraced his steps and pressed the bell. As before the ring was unanswered, and, with a quick look around, he drew out the small, steel spidery instrument.

He was somewhat quicker in his work than Tinker and, perhaps, the tiny claw entered the keyhole and emerged with a trifle more perfection of movement than the lad had been able to use, but, be that as it may, in less than ten seconds the lock was pressed back and Blake stood within the dark hall, softly closing the door after him.

What did that darkness hold? Had Tinker made a wrong move, and, as a consequence, fallen into their hands? Had this put them on their guard, and were they waiting for him, leaving the unresponsive silence to lure him along?

Now Blake knew as surely as he stood there that Green's quarry, Green himself, and most likely Tinker had entered that house not long before. If Tinker's sign was to be trusted, it certainly meant that the lad was still within it, or that something unforeseen had happened. Nothing is more eerie or suggestive of hidden menace than a pitch dark house, deadly silent in a thickly-populated district.

As Blake stood there he could hear a clock ticking near at hand. Down in the blackness of that house half a dozen pairs of hostile eyes might be peering forth, half a dozen deadly revolvers might be ready for him. He had been wary before now he redoubled his caution.

He noiselessly drew his electric torch out and held it in his left hand, his thumb on the switch. He then slipped the fingers of his right hand around the butt of his revolver and held it ready. He listened tensely for the faintest indication of human presence. He twisted his head this way and that. Nothing met him but the ticking of the clock, sounding abnormally loudly to his strained hearing.

Then slowly, ever so slowly, he put one foot forward. He pressed gently, and when no creak came he put the other forward. In this way he began moving down the black hall. His nerves were strung taut. Every muscle was tense.

What did that sinister black silence hold? What had become of Tinker? What had become of Green and the man he had followed? Whose house was it anyway, and what part did its tenants play in the affair? What was the explanation of the sign at the door which seemed to be misleading him?

He took another step —another and another. Then he stopped again and listened. Once more he moved forward, and this time his foot touched something in the dark. Withdrawing it he put out his right hand, and, hanging the revolver on his thumb by the trigger guard, felt for what it was. An overturned chair.

Instantly Blake was back, standing rigid. Then, with his revolver ready for instant work, he lifted his left hand and pressed the switch of the electric torch. In the circle of light which fell before him he saw the chair. That meant a struggle or some unusual happening. Then he threw the light about the hall.

Straight ahead he saw a half-open door, near it on the left another doorway was hung with heavy portieres, on the right was another door, and, turning, he saw three more behind him not counting the one which led into the main entrance hall of the building.

Still no sound came from around him, and, stepping over the chair, Blake moved cautiously ahead until he reached the half-open door at the end of the hall. He pushed this open and stepped inside ready for a surprise attack, but the torch soon showed it to be untenanted. He turned and switched on the light. Then he examined the room.

Almost the first thing which met his eye was a framed sketch of himself hanging on the wall. Over on the other wall was a large painting of a girl in filmy green, with deep bronze hair, standing in a garden.

The rest of the articles in the room were richly luxurious, but Blake gave his attention to the sketch and the painting. For a few brief moments he looked from one to the other, then one of his rare, slow smiles broke over his face and he put his revolver back in his pocket.

"So it is you, after all, mademoiselle," he said softly. "I thought the handling of this affair bore the earmarks of your methods, and yet I can't fathom what you have to do with Solomon Green."

He turned and passed through to the hall. From there he made a tour of every room, but not one showed signs of life, though there were many indications that human beings had been there only a short time before. The overturned chair, cigar and cigarette ashes in a small gold tray on the table in the room he had first entered, the still remaining odour of smoke, all these proved Tinker's matches had certainly led him to the right place.

But what had become of everybody, Tinker included? Since the place was Yvonne's, it argued the presence of Graves, her uncle. What had caused the sudden wholesale exodus of five or six people? They had certainly been there less than an hour ago, for he had come at once on receipt of Tinker's wire.

He shrugged his shoulders and sat down in an easy chair. A small gold fumidor half full of cigars stood on a small tabourette near him, and beside it was a decanter of whisky and a syphon of soda. With a smile reminiscent of the past, Blake took one of the cigars and lighted it, then, pouring out a portion of whisky, he added some soda.

"I'll wait an hour or two for your return, mademoiselle," he murmured. "If nothing develops by then, much as I regret doing so, I shall have to forgo any further hospitality to-night and endeavour to pick up Tinker. Unless he has fallen into your own dainty clutches I think my hopes have been well founded. This night will yield me a weapon whereby I can keep my word to Stephen Brice."

With another smile he leaned back comfortably, and after an appreciative puff at the cigar closed his eyes in thought and coolly began his wait.

For two hours Blake sat there smoking and thinking. Now that he was positive Mademoiselle Yvonne was at the bottom of the raid on Green, many little points that before had been obscure were plain. Rack his brains as he would, marshal all the facts he could bring to bear, every shred of his different analysis, he could not elucidate two cardinal points. One was the motive, the other where and how had she managed to get control of the necklace in the first place.

He considered it quite within her powers to transfer the cases themselves, even under the nose of Solomon Green. He had figured out half a dozen ways in which he could have done it himself. But it was a proved fact that Green had brought the sealed case direct from the bankers, and when he had opened it the necklace was missing. The whole explanation of the mystery rested on that one point and, turn the question which way he would, Blake could not read the riddle.

When midnight came round, and still nobody appeared, he tossed away his cigar and rose. He did not trouble to obliterate the signs of his presence, but smiled grimly as he thought: "It will give them something to worry over."

He could not imagine what had become of Tinker, and, as it was essential that he should reach more solid ground that night if he were to checkmate Green in the morning, Tinker must be found and his story heard. If the lad had discovered nothing on which to work, then Blake must return to Queen Anne's Gate, and trust to the return of Yvonne and his own powers of bluffing to gain the point he needed.

Switching out the light, he made his way along the hall and stepped out into the main entrance-hall. There was no one about, and after closing the door without any attempt at caution, he lighted a fresh cigar and started for Baker Street. A taxi soon landed him at his destination, leaving him to mount the steps with brows heavy and eyes clouded with puzzlement. On reaching the consulting-room, however, his brows went up, and he stood in the doorway, a look of amazement on his face. There, in his own big chair, sat Tinker, sound asleep, with Pedro at his feet.

The lad jumped up, and stared stupidly for a moment as Blake purposely slammed the door, then his eyes cleared and he grinned sheepishly.

"Gee, guv'nor! I was sound asleep, I guess!"

"I should have pronounced your condition as that," replied Blake drily. "Well, what explanation have you for taking me off on a wild-goose chase to Queen Anne's Gate?"

"Oh, heavens! Guv'nor, those matches! I forgot all about them; though, honestly, I had no chance to change the meaning of them by lifting one. I got into a regular hotbed of excitement there!"

"So I imagine, my lad," remarked Blake curtly. "Was it so explosive that everybody but you was blown away?"

"Ah, no! I just got away by the skin of my teeth."

"Well, well, Tinker," jerked Blake irritably, "tell me just what

78

happened. I counted on achieving much to-night, and so far, it seems to have been abortive, bar one fact— Mademoiselle Yvonne. But go on."

Tinker gazed in surprise when Blake mentioned Yvonne's name, but, in obedience to his master's command, began at once, and related every detail of his doings from the moment he had left Blake in front of Green's office, up to the moment when he reached Baker Street and discovered the black jewel-case to be empty.

"Clever —clever!" muttered Blake. "I couldn't have got the case neater myself. But you say it was empty, and yet, from the conversation you overheard between Yvonne and Green, it seems as though the necklace must have been in the case when he grabbed it. Otherwise, why were they so intent on catching him? That must be the reason of their absence. They are probably trying to head him off, thinking he may still have it."

"I've been thinking it over since I got home, guv'nor, and if I lost it after I got it from Green, there is only one occasion on which such a thing could have happened."

"Ah!" said Blake, swiftly. "When was that?"

"Well, you remember my telling you about falling over the chair when I was running down the hall?"

"Yes, yes; go on!"

"I didn't think to mention it then, but when that happened the case flew open, and I closed it as I ran. That's the only time I could possibly have lost it."

"Oh, probably! But wait. They were close after you, weren't they?"

"Yes."

"Then if you dropped it there, they must have found it. That being so, my theory that Yvonne and the others are now after Green would fall to the ground. I should have been certain to find them there when I arrived. It was too soon, after all that had happened, for the whole lot of them to leave, unless they had a very strong motive for doing so—and that motive, I felt positive, was the necklace.

"On the other hand, I know the necklace was not on the hall floor when I got there, for I made a pretty fair examination of the whole place, and particularly of that spot, for I nearly came a cropper over the same chair. No, no, no. That won't do. There is something wrong somewhere. Either my theory is all wrong, or —let me see the case!"

Tinker jumped up as Blake broke off and spoke sharply. Going to the desk, he opened a drawer and took out the black jewel-case, which he had thrust there on discovering that it was empty. He handed it to Blake, and watched closely while the detective took it across and held it under the light.

For some moments Blake studied it in silence. Finally he muttered:

"It doesn't need the pocket-glass to tell me that this is the original case all right. The marks where the cord passed over the edges are very distinct. I wonder why these corners are battered so?" (Blake did not know then that the battering was caused by Green pounding the case on his desk when he first discovered that the necklace was gone.) "It seems a perfect duplicate of the other; but, at any rate, I'll compare them."

Turning, he pulled open another drawer in the desk, and took from it the case which he had brought from Brice and Gibbs in the afternoon. Then, laying them side by side on the desk, he sat down.

Tinker's eyes widened in surprise as he saw the second case, and suddenly he recalled what he had heard Green say to Yvonne about a duplicate case.

"I say, guv'nor, is that the second case Green spoke of?" he asked quickly.

"Yes," answered Blake, smiling grimly; "and Solomon Green didn't know of its existence until I myself told him. It was that information, my lad, that formed the bait to draw him into making another move; but if we don't look sharp, all my plans will be useless!"

So saying, he bent over and picked up a thin strip of steel, marked with fine measuring lines. Then he took up the case he had received from Brice and Gibbs, and went to work.

First he measured its length to the finest measurement, next its width, and finally its depth. Then he drew a piece of paper towards him and near the left hand upper corner wrote. "Case No. 1." Underneath he jotted down the measurements he had just taken, designating them respectively by the letters "L," "W," and "D."

This done, he sprang the catch and threw back the lid. On more bringing the steel strip into use, he took the length and breadth of the interior —thus allowing for the thickness of the case itself. Jotting these down, he next measured the depth from the edge of the open cover to the point where the satin lining was set in, doing the same with the bottom. Then, after making a note of these, he thrust the case from him and drew forward the other —the one which had originally contained the necklace.

Beginning as before, he took the same three measurements while the case was closed. After that he sprang the catch and took the interior length and breadth —the fine measurements tallying to a hair with those of the other case. Then he placed the steel strip inside the cover, in order to measure the depth from the edge to where the white satin lining was fixed, and did the same to the bottom. Every measurement was the same.

He leaned back and knit his brows.

"Whoever made one made the other," he remarked, more to himself than to Tinker. "They are as alike as two peas. I've taken every measurement and —by heavens! No, I haven't, either!"

Bending forward quickly, he again drew forward case No. 1. Then he laid the steel strip outside in a perpendicular position, and took the depth from the top edge of the larger or case half to the bottom. This he jotted down. Next he measured in like manner on the lid, taking the distance from the edge which would meet the other half, when the case was closed, to the top. This he also wrote down.

Then he grasped the other case, and made similar measurements. As he put them on paper and compared them with the figures he had under No. 1, he uttered a sharp exclamation and bent forward.

"What is it, guv'nor?" asked Tinker excitedly.

"Wait, wait, until I verify my measurements!" muttered Blake.

Once more he went over his last operations, then he threw down the steel strip and pounded his clenched fist on the desk.

"Got it!" he said. "My lad, I've dropped on to one of the cleverest tricks Mademoiselle Yvonne has yet evolved!"

Quickly he drew out his pocket-glass, and picking up the case which had contained the necklace, closed it and began making a minute examination of the outside.

Around the edge he went, until he reached the back, where two tiny bulges in the leather indicated the location of the hinges. Dropping the glass, he took the case in both hands, and began manipulating the two bulges. Then he sprang the catch, the lid flew up, and Tinker gasped in amazement as he saw, lying on a white satin bed, a glittering diamond necklace, fit to grace the throat of a queen.

"Good heavens, guv'nor!" he cried. "What does it mean? Where did it come from?"

"Sit down, my lad," said Blake, lifting out the regal gems and studying them with the eye of a connoisseur. "For my own benefit as well as yours, I shall reconstruct Mademoiselle Yvonne's little game. You see these two cases?"

"Yes, guv'nor."

"I took their measurements, as you saw. Every one, as you know, tallied with the same measurement in the other. As it happened, I almost neglected the most important of the lot. In those I found a discrepancy —very small, it is true, but sufficient to arouse my suspicions. Here you see the case you got from Green. As it is now, the distances from its open-edges to the bottom and top of the case respectively tally exactly with those of the other. But, as it was before—mark this carefully, my lad—as it was before the bottom measurement of the case you got was less than that of the other and the top was more. That caused me to think.

"Then I used the glass, and what did I see? All around the top, running parallel with the edge, I saw a thin line, so faint that it was practically invisible to the naked eye, and then only if one were looking specially for it. You can see a good illustration of what I mean in a well-made fountain-pen, where the top is screwed into the barrel. In a good pen, when this is screwed in fully, only a sharp eye can pick out the line where they meet. It is the same with this case.

"I knew then what I ought to find. In a small case like this, covered by delicate leather, the spring which would open the case at that line must be concealed in a place where it could be readily manipulated, and yet not obvious to the curious. The only bulges in the leather were the two hinges at the back, and I experimented on them.

"Now watch! I close the case. I press the right hand hinge fairly in the centre. I spring the catch in front. What do you see? Nothing! The necklace has disappeared, the case is empty. I close it. I open it. The same every time.

"Now I press the left-hand spring. Voila! We open it to see the necklace, and so on. When the right-hand spring is pressed in, it automatically pushes out the other. The case then might be opened and closed a thousand times, and yet it would appear to be empty each time. On the other hand, the left spring releases the right and the necklace appears each time.

"The two compartments are lined the same, and are identical in appearance. The measurements are so fine and the work, so accurately done that it would pass without arousing suspicion nearly every time.

"And that is how Yvonne worked it, for that she was the young widow who posed as Mrs. Carter, I now know. The necklace was in the case all the time. When she took it from Green in his office this morning, on the pretence of examining the seal, she simply pressed the right-hand spring, and, of course, when Green opened it the case is empty, or apparently so. Then between there and the Bank she managed to make the transfer, and that is how it came about that Green entered the bank with a different case.

"It is remarkably simple, and yet the biggest mysteries are usually capable of a most ordinary explanation. I don't know yet what part the share certificates play in the matter, nor what this man you say is called Bayes has to do with Yvonne. Whatever the explanation of those two points will give us the motive. I feel sure.

"And now, my lad, to bed. We shall be busy to-morrow morning."

Tinker rose, and, with a wondering shake of the head, departed while Blake filled his pipe, and, with the necklace on his knees, fell to dreaming.

Sexton Blake gazed long and intently
at his own portrait.

The Eighth Chapter.   Blake Visits Yvonne —The Web —The End.

MADEMOISELLE YVONNE returned to Queen Anne's Gate just as day was breaking. She had left the Honourable Algy at his club, and made her way home weary and disappointed. She had spent hours on the watch at Green's office, but he had not put in an appearance. She was hoping against hope that Graves and Alec would head him off at his home, and thought thoroughly fagged, sat down to await their return.

They came in less than half an hour later to report their non-success, and Yvonne, too weary to hold a council of war then, dismissed them, and made her way to bed.

The truth of the matter was that Green, thoroughly alarmed by the mysterious jerking of the case from his hand as he raced along the hall, and frightened his act might land him within the toils of the law—for he now felt assured Yvonne was quite clever enough to accomplish that —had sped along until he saw a taxi, and leaping in, had been driven direct to his home. Consequently, he was there all the time Graves and Alec had been waiting for him.

It was past eight o'clock when Yvonne's maid brought in her tea, drew the curtains, and laid out her toilet articles. At half-past eight Yvonne, looking as freshly charming as though had slept for hours, was at breakfast, exercising her pretty head over the mystifying events of the previous night.

Then it was that the bell rang, and a moment later the housemaid appeared, bearing on a small tray a card. Yvonne picked it up, wondering who could be calling at such an early hour, but as she read the name she uttered a sharp ejaculation which caused Graves to look up quickly from his paper.

"What is it?" he asked.

For answer Yvonne passed over the card.

"Good heavens, Sexton Blake!" he muttered.

"Will you see him?"

"Of course," she replied, with a faint shrug.

Then, turning to her maid, she said:

"Show Mr. Blake in, Anna. Tell him I shall be with him in a moment."

For five minutes she sat rigid in thought, then, with half-veiled eyes, she tripped along and entered the reception-room. Blake rose at once, and put out both his hands. Holding hers fast, he drew her over to the window and looked humorously into the wistful eyes, which were glinting in the light with a myriad soft violet flecks.

"Why did you do it?" he asked, still retaining her hands.

She laughed deliciously.

"How did you know?"

Blake smiled faintly.

"How do I usually know?" he said. "Are you always going to run these risks?"

Yvonne wriggled her right hand free, and laid it on his shoulder. Then she looked at him.

"There was nothing wrong this time," she said softly. "You would have done as much yourself. Come into the breakfast-room, and I'll tell you everything if you will tell me how you discovered me."

Blake smiled, and recovered her hand.

"It is a bargain. I am most anxious to know about those shares," he said softly.

•   •   •   •   •   •

Stephen Brice and his partner sat in moody silence on either side of the desk of the former. It was nine-thirty in the morning, and so far they had heard nothing from Blake since he had departed the day before, with the stated intention of calling upon Solomon Green.

The bank would open soon, and if the promoter kept his threat, by noon the old banking firm of Brice & Gibbs would be swept away in that wrecker of business —rumour. They had long ago exhausted every plan to escape the deluge, and were now apathetically waiting for the blow to fall.

It wanted just a few minutes to ten when a knock came at the private entrance by which the partners were accustomed to arrive and leave. Gibbs rose wearily, and went to answer it. He stared in astonishment as he saw quite a little crowd collected outside, and before he could make any remark they, had all pushed their way in.

Blake and Yvonne were the first to enter, and behind them came Tinker, Pedro, Graves, and the Honourable Algernon Bayes. Disregarding the look of astonishment on the faces of the partners, Blake went straight to the point.

"Has Green made a move yet?" he asked, turning to Gibbs.

"No; but he will at ten o'clock."

"Good! Where does that door open into?" went on Blake, indicating a door on the right.

"An unused office."

"Excellent! Mademoiselle, will you and the others please go in there?"

As they turned away Blake faced round again to the partners.

"Get some money ready—fifty thousand. When Green comes, have him in here. If he still persists in demanding the money, pay him; don't mistake me—pay him. There isn't time to explain now, but I promise if he does take the money he won't get away with it, nor will you suffer in any way. I've got everything just where I want it.

"I shall leave the door of that office ajar in order to hear. Go ahead as though I weren't there at all. When the proper moment arrives I'll come out and take matters into my own hands. Will you do this?"

They both nodded.

"Yes," answered Gibbs. "There is nothing else to do." Blake turned at once and sought the room where the others were concealed just as ten o'clock struck. Almost on the last stroke a clerk entered and informed Brice that Solomon Green desired an interview, and a moment later he was shown in, looking a trifle pale from the excitement of the night before, but none the less determined to bleed the bankers for the fifty thousand.

"Well," he demanded suavely, "have you found my clients necklace?"

"No, Mr. Green," replied Brice, rising to the occasion. "I am sorry to say we haven't."

"Then I presume you are prepared to pay me the cash value of it?"

"We are not, Mr. Green. Firstly, we feel confident the necklace was in the case when it was handed to you, and, secondly, we would not care to pay the value of it, until you brought your client in person."

"Then, by heavens, you can consider my account withdrawn. Inside an hour the whole City will know how reliable Brice & Gibbs are!"

"Those are strong measures to take, Mr. Green."

"Maybe they are, but I'll take them. Come! Pay over the fifty thousand, and not only will I keep mum but I'll leave my account here just the same."

"In a word, to avoid ruin we must pay you that amount?" interposed Gibbs.

"You couldn't have stated it better," answered Green.

"Then I think we had better pay it, Stephen," went on the junior partner.

"Very well," remarked Brice. "Will you get the cash?"

Blake could well imagine the gleam of triumph in Green's eyes during the silence that followed while Gibbs got the money and passed it over. Then he heard the Jew's voice again.

"I shall not count it. It is sure to be correct."

"Rather anxious to get away with it, aren't you?" came a drawling voice from behind Green. And he turned to find himself gazing into the black muzzle of an automatic, behind which smiled the countenance of Sexton Blake. "Just put those notes back on the table, Mr. Green," went on Blake, advancing into the room. "Quick!"

And at the sharp command, Green dropped them.

"What does this mean?" he demanded thickly.

"It means, my clever and elusive friend, that for once in your life you have overreached yourself," replied Blake, coolly gathering up the notes and tossing them over to Brice. "You have just gone the full length in a case of blackmail, Mr. Green, and I think you know what that means."

"Blackmail," blustered Green. "What do you mean? I'm collecting this money to pay my client for the necklace which the bank has lost."

Blake turned.

"Mrs. Carter!" he called.

In answer another figure appeared through the doorway behind Green. She was garbed in black from head to foot, her features were covered by a black veil, and on her left hand, which was bare of glove, shone a very new wedding-ring.

Green's eyes threatened to leave his head as he saw his former client approaching him.

"Mrs. Carter," said Blake, "this man says you have lost a valuable diamond necklace which was left here for safe keeping. Is that so?"

"Why, no!" came in clear tones from behind the veil. "I have my necklace quite safely. See, here it is!"

As she spoke she threw up her veil, and from beneath the jacket drew a black jewel-case. Springing the catch, she revealed to the astonished Green, as well as to the partners, a glittering string of diamonds lying against the white satin.

"You see you are quite wrong, Mr. Green," drawled Blake.

"Then where is the money I advanced on them?" blazed Green, half-rising.

"Why, I paid you back," replied Yvonne in simulated surprise. "Didn't you receive twenty-five thousand pounds' worth of share certificates in your own company? Surely you cannot deny that?"

"You know they are worth nothing," growled the Jew.

"Indeed! One moment."

Yvonne turned and called:

"Mr. Bayes!"

The Honourable Algy appeared.

"Mr. Bayes," went on Yvonne, "did I understand you to say that Mr. Green told you no later than yesterday afternoon that the Golden Princess Mine had struck it very rich?"

"Rather," replied the Honourable Algy. "You know you did, Green. Up at the club. More than that, you tried to sell me some more stock in it."

And then Green, seeing the web which Sexton Blake had woven for him, leaped to his feet, and turned on the detective. "Curse you!" he cried. "I owe this to you. I'll get even with you for this if it takes me ten years. And you —you—" he stuttered, swinging on Yvonne.

But what he intended to say will never be known, for just as Blake leaped forward, the Honourable Algy drove a straight-right which caught the Jew on the point of the jaw, and sent him spinning. Blake grasped him as he reeled, and, opening the door, propelled him into the outer office. Then, lighting a cigar, he said:

"Really, my friends, if I were in your place I'd push that gentleman for blackmail. You've got a magnificent case and unimpeachable witnesses." And he smiled at Yvonne.

Graves, Tinker, and Pedro had entered, and the whole party sat down to discuss the question, the partners finally deciding to content themselves by closing Green's account and avoiding any further publicity.

Then Blake rose.

"All right. I don't know but what you are wise," he said.

Then he turned to the others.

"I don't know what you are going to do," he said, with a smile, "but I am going to the Venetia for an early lunch, and Mademoiselle Yvonne is coming with me. Come along, mademoiselle. Au revoir."

And they disappeared on their way to enjoy a pleasant hour at the Venetia —an hour into which we shall not intrude.

THE END.

[33300 WORDS]

Sexton Blake solving the riddle of the jewel-cases.

PLAYING THE GAME.

Two Scots met in a golf match. On one side of the course there was a high railway embankment. Over this railway it happened Jock drove his ball.

They hunted for it a long time, but could not find it.

Sandy wanted Jock to give it up; but Jock wouldna, for a lost ball means a lost hole.

Finally, Jock took a new ball frae his poke, dirtied it, and pretended to find it.

"Here 'tis, Sandy!" he called.

"Ye're a leear, Jock!" responded Sandy.

"I'm no a leear! Here 'tis!"

"Ye're a leear, for I've had it in ma pocket for fufteen meenits!"

ANOTHER BEAUTY CURE.

A lady had in her employ an excellent maid who had but one fault —her face was always smudged.

Her mistress tried to tell her without causing offence to wash her face.

"Do you know, Jane." she remarked, "that if you wash your face every day in hot, soapy water it will make you beautiful?"

"Shure, it's a wonder ye niver tried it; ma'am," was the startling reply.

DIDN'T COUNT.

Two Irishmen arranged to fight a duel with pistols. One of them was distinctly stout, and when he saw his lean adversary facing him he raised an objection.

"Bedad," he said, "I'm twice as big a target as he is, so I ought to stand twice as far away from him as he is from me."

"Be aisy now," replied his second. "I'll soon put that right."

Taking a piece of chalk from his pocket, he drew two lines down the stout man's coat, leaving a space between them.

"Now," he said, turning to the other man, "fire away, ye spalpeen, and remember that any hits outside that chalk line don't count."

VERY REFINED

He had told her, of course, that he was heir to a marquisate, and, whether it was true or not, there is no doubt that she regarded him as the quintessence of politeness. They had had a meal at the Cafe Macaroni one night, and she was favouring a bosom friend with the details next day.

"Yes; he took me off ter supper at a reg'lar rest'rant last night."

"They tell me he's real refined?"

"Rarver! When he poured his coffee out in 'is saucer ter cool it, he didn't blow it like some common people would, but fanned it wid 'is 'at."

STILL "TO LET."

Flat Agent: "That's the servant's bed-room, and this is the linen cupboard,"

Prospective Tenant: "I see; the cupboard is the one with shelves in it."

COLONEL SCOTCHEM had had at very arduous day retreating from the enemy, and he wished to recoup his strength in order that he might retreat still further on the morrow.

"MacPherson," he said to his new servant, "I'm going to snatch forty winks' sleep. Stay by my tent, and see that I'm not disturbed."

Mac saluted. Five minutes later the snores of Colonel Scotchem were cut short by the loud report of a gun.

"Mercy me!" cried the colonel. "Are the enemy upon us?"

"Na, dinna fret," replied Mac, inserting his head reassuringly through the tent-flap. "It was only a wee mouse. But as I thought he might wake you up I shot him."

DICK OF THE HIGHWAYS.

By DAVID GOODWIN.

SHORT INTRODUCTION FOR NEW READERS.

Dick Langley's brother, spendthrift and waster, loses at a throw of the dice all the money and estates of the Langleys to a scoundrel named Sir Mostyn Frayne, and afterwards shoots himself. Dick Langley is thus left penniless and alone. Circumstances over which he has no control compel him to take to the road. A reward is offered for his apprehension. Dick holds up two travellers, and one of them doubts the make of Dick's pistol.

Now Go On.

The Miser of Barton.

"The pistol is no doubt admirable," he said; "though whether it is a true Joe Manton I doubt. If you will lend it to me a moment, I will soon tell you!"

Dick Langley, for it was he, smiled serenely.

"I can assure you of its genuineness," he said. "And it has another peculiarity. If anybody at whom it is presented does not produce his

93

purse within two minutes, it invariably goes off. One minute and a half have already passed."

"Oh, my dear master!" broke out the elder traveller, addressing his young companion. "Pray surrender him your purse without delay! What are a few guineas to your precious life? Ah, me, I could never serve another if you, the last of your family, were killed!"

The young man's face was a study. He looked sourly for a moment at his companion, who wore the impression of a faithful servant advising a young master. The young man drew out reluctantly a purse full of guineas, and handed it to the highwayman.

Dick Langley took it with a bow, and glanced at the other traveller.

"You are a prudent fellow," he said waggishly. "Are you, then, a servant and adviser to this gentleman?"

"I am his humble retainer, and a man of peace," said the elder man cringingly. "I have nothing about me worth your honour's attention; but if you wish—"

"No, no," said Dick, curtly, "I pluck only those who can spare the money, and you are safe enough, for me. Now, sir, you may ride on about your business with my deepest apologies for having delayed you."

The two travellers, the younger one looking very sour indeed, touched their horses and went on their way.

Dick rode onwards rather pensively; he was sorry he had stopped the two men at all. There was something about the younger of the two travellers that he liked.

After awhile, he turned his mare and went back after them. A sudden resolve had come upon him to return the young man's purse. But he failed, for he came to three cross-roads, and not knowing which, they had taken—there were too many hoof-marks to trace them —he took the wrong one.

"Methinks that lad was not so wealthy after all, and couldn't spare the money," he said. "If I can discover his name, I will certainly return it to him."

It was late in the day when, some miles to the northward, Dick approached a small hamlet that was well known to him, and came upon a figure he recognised —a poacher —Dick had little love of poachers, but he had some regard for this one, and called out to the man.

"Hallo, Steve, you rascal! You've been poaching! There's a hare inside that jacket of yours, I'll warrant!"

Steve Dowsing was a young villager in very ragged clothes, who looked as if he had never had enough to eat. Which was perfectly correct; he had not.

"Ay, sir," he said, touching his cap—for Dick had befriended him once already. "I've got an owd 'are buttoned under me jacket; an' a good job, too, or mother wouldn't get her supper to-night. You stops the gentlemen, you see, an' I stops their game. You didn't get much out o' owd Henry Graham this morning though, I was lyin' up in the copse for a pheasant an' heard the whole thing. Ho! Ho! Excuse me, sir, but he took you in fine!"

"What do you mean, Steve? His purse was not princely, indeed, but well filled enough for a prosperous young lawyer, as I take him to be. What is he —a duke in disguise, then?"

"Nay, I don't mean the young gentleman. Owd Graham, in the rusty cloak," said Steve, chuckling.

"What, the serving-man?"

"He's no serving-man, sir? That's Henry Graham, the young gentleman's uncle, an' worth fifty times what he'll ever be. An' I know he'd been to Cleabury Bank that morning, and had most like a couple o' hundred guineas about him. He played the servant to save his gold. I'd ha' come out, and told you, only I daren't meddle in a hangin' matter."

"'Od's blood!" said Dick, clenching his bridle-hand, "did the old sinner befool me, then?" His brow cleared, and he broke into a laugh. "It was cleverly done. Well, the youngster will get his money back from his uncle, then, of course. The old man will be well pleased at having saved the rest. I would not have touched the nephew's purse had I known."

"You don't know Henry Graham, sir," said Steve, with a bitter smile. "It's little o' that money his nephew'll see,"

"What!" said Dick, growing angry again, "do you mean to tell me he wouldn't—"

"Ay, I do. Have you never heard o' the Miser o' Barton Ferris, sir?" returned Steve.

"Yes, I've heard of him."

"Well, Henry Graham's he, an' may the curse light on him! That man, sir, ha' got more 'guineas hidden in his house at Barton than there are drops in the pond there, an' he's the meanest owd villain in the country. He washes in gold o' nights, they say, an' sartain there's loads of it there. But only he knows where it's hid. Robbers broke in once and left him for dead, but they didn't find the bulk of the gold.

"He starves himself rather than spend, an' he's the cruellest man to deal with alive. He's the landlord o' our bit o' cottage, where my mother lives. Two years ago I was out o' work —she depends on me, you see—an' behind two weeks with the rent. Graham comes to me, and gives me the choice of signing a new lease, bindin' me to do four days' work a week for him for nothin', by way of rent, or being turned out.

"My mother was well at the time, an' I had to sign. She's bedridden now, an' can't be moved, and I can't get the lease altered. He's got me tight, and gets four days' a week for two-and-sixpence rent. Result is, I can't get work nowheres else, an' we both of us starves. It's only by this poachin' that I'm drove to, that we keep alive at all. An' we're only one family of a dozen that he grinds down to starvation to fill his money-bags an' gloat over."

"Can such things be?" said Dick, his eyes blazing. "Tell me quickly where does this man live?"

"Barton Ferris Hall, a big owd house, very lonely, an' broken-up-like, two mile down the lane past the Village."

"Does his nephew lodge with him?"

"Lodge with Graham? He wouldn't give a crust to his own brother if he was d'yin'! His nephew lodges at the Barton Inn. There's nobody at the hall but one old body-servant that Graham keeps to do the rent-collecting and dirty work for him."

"Be at your cottage to-night, Steve, about eight," said Dick grimly. "I shall want you. Here's a guinea for you. Mr. Henry Graham is about to learn a lesson he will never forget."

The Miser and the Horse-Pistol.

It was very dark, and the rain swept over the fields in sharp squalls before a driving wind.

The gaunt old house of Ferris Hall looked particularly gloomy on that winter night, and about half-past seven o'clock the outer gate was opened, and a bent old woman hobbled feebly to the door of the house and knocked. She was wrapped in a black cloak, tattered and stained, and it was some time before she got any answer.

At last a step sounded inside, the door was opened an inch, or less, and a low voice growled, "Who's there?"

"It's only old Mrs. White, with her rent," whined the old woman.

"Well, this ain't the time to bring it!" growled the voice.

"Ay, but I can't get it off my mind!" said the old woman; "an' I've come to see if Mr. Graham won't let me have a shilling of it back till next time, for my husband's dyin', and he—"

"No; he won't let you have, no shillin'!" snapped the manservant, opening the door a little. "It's about time old White did die, for his lease ends with him, an' we can get a better tenant, an' raise the rent. Give it here, as you've brought it. Blood and hounds!"

He winced and flung up his arm, for the old woman's cloak dropped, and the form of Dick Langley stood before him. A cocked pistol stared the manservant in the face, and he trembled, dumbstruck.

"I am not pleased with you, Mr. Steward," said Dick, "I do not like your way of doing business. Move and you are a dead man!"

The steward dared not utter a word; and Dick, seizing a scarf, stuffed it into the man's open mouth as a gag, and bound his wrists behind him. Then he entered the hall, led the man to a cupboard that was standing open, tied the man's feet that he might not kick and raise an alarm, and thrust him in.

"If you make the least noise," he said, as he turned the key on him, "it will be your last."

Dick pocketed the key and walked noiselessly into the house. He wanted very badly to find Mr. Graham.

At first his search was fruitless. The great, lonely house, now that the manservant was safely stowed in the cupboard, seemed lifeless as a vault, and not a light could be seen anywhere. Dick groped his way about as best he could, and presently went down to the ground-floor.

There, at last, he saw a faint light showing through a chink at the end of a cold brickwork passage.

"That will be Mr. Graham amusing himself with his gains," thought Dick.

He crept up to the door and listened. The musical chink of coins greeted him, and occasionally a low, dry chuckle.

He felt the door all over, giving most attention to the lock. The key was turned, but he decided the door would give way to a heavy blow.

He retired some distance, took a run, and charged the door with his shoulder, putting all his weight into the rush. The door burst open with a crash. There was a wild cry, a clatter of coins, and Dick found himself in a small, bare room, faced by the miser, who had darted up from his seat at a table laden with golden guineas, and was quivering with rage and fright.

Dick's horse-pistol covered him in a moment.

"Fill your pockets with that gold!" ordered the young highwayman; "fill them to the brim, and cram as much more into your wallet. Then come with me. Quick!"

"Robber! Assassin!" screamed Graham, loud and trembling. "I defy you! I will die first!"

He flung himself on the table and embraced his beloved money with both arms.

Dick stepped forward, and the cold muzzle of the pistol pressed against the miser's neck. The shock seemed to sober him.

"Decide quickly!" said Dick. "If you do not obey, I will shoot you like a dog, and distribute your wealth to the poor. You are not fit to live. Choose swiftly, obedience or death!"

There was a pause, and the miser rose. His face was the face of a man in torture; but he grasped handfuls of guineas, and stuffed them into his pockets and wallet till they could hold no more. What this meant he did not know; he only knew he was going to lose them.

"Walk out before me," said Dick, "and, remember, one false step, one treacherous move, and you are a dead man!" He marched the miser out of the house, and away into the windy dark. Graham, the pistol always at his back, walked as one in a dream. Presently a light shone ahead. It was Steve Dowsing's cottage. Dick made his prisoner open the door, and walked him in.

Old Mrs. Dowsing, on her couch in the corner, and her son stared as though they saw a ghost.

"Good-evening, dame!" said Dick. "Steve, I told you I should want you. And now, Mr. Graham, I will explain. You suffer from the vice of avarice, and you have mercilessly trodden down the poor over whom you have power, to gratify your lust for hoarding gold. These are two very ugly faults. I intend teaching you a lesson to-night."

The miser stared stupidly. He could scarcely take his eyes from the threatening pistol. Steve and his mother were not less astonished.

"We will begin here," said Dick: "You will remit on the spot, the last two years' rent of this cottage. That comes to thirteen guineas.

Count them out and hand them to Steve Dowsing."

It was done.

"Now, sit down. Pen, ink, and paper, Steve, if you have them. Mr. Graham will grant a lease of the cottage at two shillings a week for three years. That is a fair rent. Sign it, please. Excellent! By this the former lease is cancelled."

Steve and his mother broke into heartfelt gratitude; but Dick stopped them hurriedly.

"Come, Steve," he said, "I want you to guide me and Mr. Graham to all his other tenants. After that we will visit the poor of the neighbourhood."

Henry Graham was not sure whether that journey was a nightmare or a terrible reality. With the inexorable pistol at his back, and Steve Dowsing trotting alongside to show Dick the way, he was marched round to all the cottages in the vicinity.

His beloved money, of which his pockets and wallet were full, flowed like water. He felt as though he was parting with the very blood from his veins. Here, a poor cottager was relieved, there a starving family received a handful of guineas, and yonder a new and easier lease was granted and signed by him.

Whenever he hesitated the cold pistol-muzzle gave him warning to hasten. Steve Dowsing led the way, and showed the houses of those in need; Dick decided the sum his prisoner was to hand out. At last, when the last guinea was given away, Graham was marched back to his house.

Then Dick Langley mounted the black mare and rode on his way. And the Miser of Barton Ferris was left biting his nails on his own doorstep, wondering if he were asleep or awake.

"It gave me a very keen pleasure to settle accounts with that skinflint," said the young highwayman to himself, as he spurred out across the wide heaths beyond Barton. "I think I shall be none the less popular for it hereabouts. Such a man can have few friends, nor do I fear that he will dare set the Riders at me —not that they will catch me if he does. I have a mind to tarry awhile in Barton Ferris, for I marked a very good inn by the cross-roads, which is kept by one who was once a tenant of mine. Let us see, Kitty, whether he keeps good cheer."

And so saying, Dick rode forth to the Hare and Hounds, at Barton, where he found excellent quarters, and lay quiet and snug there for four full days and nights.

The Three Bad Guineas.

"Well, host, why such a long face? Have you been caught watering the ale?"

The landlord of the Hare and Hounds, at Barton Ferris, was striding in his tap-room, and looking with a gloomy visage at the three guinea-pieces which were nailed to the counter, just as Dick Langley entered the inn, after a ride for pleasure through the lonely beech-woods.

"Why, I doubt not that I wear sour enough face this evening, sir," he said, "for, look you, 'tis a heavy loss for a poor man. There be three guineas I have given good silver for, to say nothing o' wine and a pair o' fat capons, and not one o' the three is fit for ought but a nail through its middle. And my brewer's score is due, too, and the good wife sick. I know not where to turn to pay the doctor, now."

"Tut, tut, man; is it as bad as that?" said Dick, looking closely at the coins. "Ay, bad coins, sure enough, and cleverly made, too. Some knave has treated you very ill, landlord. No matter, here are three that ring true enough, I'll warrant. Nay, man, take them; you need them more than I."

"Bless you sir!" said the worthy innkeeper almost in tears with gratitude. "I'll take them then, though I would not were things less bad with me. Ah, you're a good friend to the poor, Master D—"

"Sh!" said Dick, under his breath, with a warning glance.

And the landlord checked himself rather hastily, looking as though he could have bitten his tongue out, for there was a stranger in the room.

"A dirty trade —coining," said Dick. "A knave's trick, in truth. A chicken stealer is an honest man to a coiner, me-thinks."

"You say truly, sir," said the stranger sitting behind him.

He was a big, powerful man, well but plainly dressed, with a keen, but honest and frank face. Dick, who had hardly noticed him at first, knew him now, for a King's agent —a man who in these days would be a chief inspector of police.

Dick wondered for a moment if he had walked into a trap; but the man did not recognise him, and, in fact, like most people, took Dick, by his clothes and manner, to be what he was before Sir Mostyn Frayne's villainy had ruined him and driven him to the road —a wealthy, and hard-riding young landowner.

"We agree, it seems," said Dick, with a cheery smile. "I hope," he added, with a keen glance at the man, "you will bring the knaves to book. I like not to see bad money about."

"You have guessed my business," laughed the stranger. "Well, sir, I hope soon to succeed —sooner than the rogues think, perhaps. But I will say no more."

"Success to you!" said Dick.

And they pledged each other. Then the King's Rider went out and rode away.

Dick stayed a little longer, listening to the landlord's stories of the amount of bad money in the district, and his belief that it was made not far away. Then Dick left the inn, mounted Black Kitty, and trotted along the highway. He followed the road where it led through the thickets of Barton Woods, and slowed to a walk.

"Egad, Kitty!" he said to the mare. "I never drank a toast more heartily than that to the King's man. It would be bad for you and me, lass, if we took purses with naught but forged guineas in them. Softly! There's someone riding ahead. Is it a prize? No; our friend of the inn, by St, George! It is a task well spiced with danger, I warrant, hunting down these rogues of coiners, for they are cunning rascals, and do not boggle at a murder or so."

In the twilight ahead, sure enough, the big King's Rider was walking his sturdy chestnut along at a slow pace. Kitty stepped so lightly on the turf by the roadside that the horseman did not look round.

"Nay, Kitty," whispered Dick. "he may have a purse of guineas about him, but he could ill spare them, and he earns them hard. None except the rich and miserly have reason to fear us. But, gadzooks, there is someone following him! An ill-looking knave, too!"

Silently as a ghost, a dim figure on foot slipped out of the thickets, and tiptoed softly behind the unsuspecting horseman. In his hand was a heavy bludgeon, and one glance was enough to show that he meant mischief.

"Egad," thought Dick, "there's murder in the wind here! 'Tis one of the rascals he is hunting, no doubt, and the knave has waylaid him! A King's man is my enemy, but pink me if I'll see a man struck down from behind!"

The horseman rode on, suspecting no evil, and the ruffian stole

101

after him, intent on his task. He was nearly up to his quarry now. Dick touched Kitty on the flank, and sent her along faster till she was within a dozen yards of the man with the club. Neither stalker nor stalked heard her velvety tread.

Three more paces, and the murderer was right behind his victim. He raised his bludgeon to strike.

Dick sent Kitty leaping forward in two great bounds, and before the bludgeon could fall he sent its owner rolling on the turf with a blow of his pistol-butt.

"A thousand devils!" cried the King's man, turning sharply, and whipping out a pistol. "What now?"

"Why, sir," said Dick coolly, pointing to the rogue who was rolling, half-stunned, upon the grass, "I saw this knave about to try the weight of that bludgeon on your skull, so I tried my pistol-butt on his. If I'm not mistaken, it will be one of the gang you're after!"

"Gadzooks! It is, indeed!" cried the horseman, springing down and pinning the fellow.

The knave tried to resist, but the powerful captor overcame him easily, bound his wrists behind him, and attached the rope to his saddle-bow for a lead.

"It is a poor return making speeches, when you have saved my life, sir," he said heartily to Dick. "You have done me a double service. I was keeping a bad look-out while thinking over my plans. It will not be long now ere I have the rest. I trust the time will come, sir, when I can repay the good turn you have done me."

"A mere nothing," said Dick, with a cheery laugh. "Say no more about it."

"I never forget a service," said the other. "And now, a kindly good-night to you, sir, while I take this rogue into safe keeping. Might I know your name?"

"Let it keep till our next meeting," said Dick with a smile; "you may, perhaps, hear it 'twixt then and now."

"'Tis the name of a gentleman, I'll be sworn," said the other. "Good-night to you, and a safe journey."

He rode away, and his prisoner went with him, led by a rope, and cursing and growling savagely under his breath.

Dick put Kitty to the trot, and passed in the opposite direction.

"Faith, a little adventure is well enough," said Dick; "but I must take a goodly purse or two to-night, or I shall find myself with empty coffers. And, after all, this road through the thickets leads to two towns, and should be as good a place as any to find a fat merchant on his travels, or a squire with a fob full of guineas.

Dick patrolled the road for a couple of hours, but not a soul passed. At last he walked Kitty for the third time through a defile, where the road ran between bushy knolls and cliffs and banks of sandstone.

(Another fine long Instalment next week.)

"THE WHITE MANDARIN."

"THE WHITE MANDARIN," next week's Wu Ling versus Sexton Blake yarn, promises well, my chums. It deals with one of the most daring plots ever devised.

The ingenious method employed by Wu Ling is characteristic of him, and his great machine, the Brotherhood of the Yellow Beetle, carries out his plans perfectly, and once again Wu Ling fancies he has the upper hand.

But Sexton Blake once more proves his superior powers. He not only stops the tea conspiracy, but carries the war right into China itself, and there poses as a wealthy mandarin. His perils and adventures are vividly set forth, and I predict a phenomenal success for "The White Mandarin."

A LETTER OF INTEREST.

Here is a letter which carries with it a deal of interest, my chums. I think all will agree with me that it is good of our chum, W. J. Baker, to write such a fine letter to us, and that he deserves great success in his business, of which he speaks.

"*Learmonth,*
"*Victoria,*
"*Australia.*
"*July 12, 1913.*

"*Dear Skipper,—After just finishing reading one of your splendid yarns, I feel that I must thank you sincerely for placing such enthralling literature upon the market.*

"*Since I was first able to read, and understand what I read, I have been—to use a phrase commonly used by all who knew me— 'a beggar for books' and I must say that my friends were right, for I have* devoured with my eyes every form of literature I could obtain, and amongst other books I have come across the UNION JACK.

"At first I only liked the yarns, and wished for more of 'Sexton Blake.' This, I might mention, was when 'Blake' yarns only appeared periodically; but as he began to occupy every issue of the paper, my interest grew, and I looked out for more about this great character, until now I am quite content to let all other literature go and stick to the old JACK.

"I cannot tell you, Skipper, the exact date of my first meeting with your paper, but suffice to say that I have read of the exploits of Sexton Blake & Co. under my desk at school, and on leaving and seeking my own living. I read of him again whilst on errands as parcels boy at a big drapery establishment in Castlemaine. Leaving that occupation, I obtained a position with a pastrycook, and again in my spare time I devoured the UNION JACK, and so right on from one job to another, until now I am the proud owner of a small business of my own. I have made Sexton Blake my hero, and the pleasure I have derived from reading of his adventures, and how, with the help of Tinker and Pedro, he has time and again upheld the fact that the law must be obeyed and that all wrong-doers must in the end pay the penalty of their misdeeds.

"Scores of times I have had it pointed out to me that those 'penny horrors' as the UNION JACK has insultingly been called in common with other novels, contained harmful reading, but I have indignantly denied the fact, and am proud to say that not one of its condemners has had a leg to stand upon when I have quietly asked them to try a copy, and on reading it have had to confess that it really was a splendid paper.

"I remember one incident. My Sunday School teacher once noticed the JACK sticking out of my pocket during class, and began to condemn the book at once. The class took sides, and a debate ensued, our defence being a denial that because a book had only paper covers and cost only a small sum, that it was not fit matter to be read by anyone, and I asked my teacher, a deeply religious man, to read a copy I gave him, and if then he considered the book unfit for reading I would stop reading it, and apologise to him for the stand I took.

"He read it, and instead of me having to apologise, he did, and the outcome of that little incident gained the book three or four new readers, himself among the number.

"My late father was an enthusiastic reader also, and I can honestly say that nowhere have I seen such interest displayed over a book as I have over the UNION JACK.

"The good I have myself obtained from reading it, no one can know, but it has been a good friend to me, and the variety of the yarns makes it all the more popular. I have read the opinion of many loyal readers, and can only add that I trust Sexton Blake will long uphold the principle for which he stands, and continue as the leading character in the foremost book of the period, preeminent above all others, the UNION JACK.

"Sincerely yours,

*"*W. J. BAKER.*"*

A BIG O.K.!

The following letter tells us what "BRONCHO" thinks of the old paper. Many thanks "Broncho."

"Toronto, Ontario.

"Canada.

"July 1913.

"Dear Skipper,—It is with the greatest of pleasure that I write regarding the UNION JACK, *and I might say that I have been a reader of the paper for some considerable time, while most of them do certainly contain some clever ideas regarding the detection of crime.*

"I am an Englishman, having been out here just a year, and I may say that I am getting on fine, and since I have been out here, I have read some of the American detective yarns, but give me the good old UNION JACK, *and I am satisfied.*

"There is one thing I should like to ask you, and that is. 'Are the Sexton Blakes we get out here written and printed here?' because I have very often noticed Canadian expressions in the conversation of the actors of the story-dramas; this I did not notice in the Old Country."

*(No, my chum, they are all printed in the Old Country.—*THE SKIPPER.)

"I have just finished reading the story 'The Idol's Spell.' an adventure with the Brotherhood of the Yellow Beetle and I will tell you right here that it was a splendid yarn, full of cleverness and excitement from start to finish, and if you give us such grand stories as that the UNION JACK *will very soon be the*

"MASTERPIECE OF DETECTIVE LITERATURE.

"*I might add that Yvonne was a splendid character, a girl worthy of the great detective, for I can tell you right here that a detective can love, for she is certainly some class, in all that I have read of her.*

"*The Plummer and Carlac yarns are also a big 'O.K.,' and I am waiting for the big Summer Number, which I know will be of the best.*

"*With these few remarks I will bring my letter to a close, at the same time wishing you and the good old* UNION JACK *every success, the latter which I am passing on to my Canadian friends.*

"*Believe me to be, Yours faithfully,*

"BRONCHO."

DO IT STRAIGHT!

As all my chums know, I never use these columns as a medium for "sermons" and such, but the following little poem struck me as being very short, sweet, and true. Learn it off by heart, and keep it in your mind. It will be useful, I am sure:

HONESTY.
"There is only one good way—
Do it straight.
And it pays best every day—
Do it straight.
If you want to make a name,
If you want to play a game,
If it's money, just the same—
Do it straight.

"If you've anything to say,
Say it straight.
It's the only decent way—
Say it straight.
Though perhaps you seem to lose,
It's the manly part to choose.
Down with sneaking, 'shady' views—
And be straight!"

THE SKIPPER.

Printed and published weekly by the Proprietors, at The Fleetway House, Farringdon Street, London, England. Subscription, 7a, per annum. Agents for Australia; Gordon & Gotch, Melbourne, Sydney, Adelaide, Brisbane; and Wellington, N.Z. South Africa: The Central News Agency, Ltd., Cape Town and Johannesburg Saturday. September 13, 1913.

www.ingramcontent.com/pod-product-compliance
Lightning Source LLC
Chambersburg PA
CBHW031851170626
46807CB00004B/1669